Book Two

Part Three

Phantoms In Pursuit

by

S. L. Howarth

ISBN: 978-1-326-00630-3

Copyright © 2014 S. L. Howarth

All rights reserved, including the right to reproduce this book, or portions thereof in any form. No part of this text may be reproduced, transmitted, downloaded, decompiled, reverse engineered, or stored, in any form or introduced into any information storage and retrieval system, in any form or by any means, whether electronic or mechanical without the express written permission of the author.

This is a work of fiction. Names and characters are the product of the author's imagination and any resemblance to actual persons, living or dead, is entirely coincidental.

PublishNation, London
www.publishnation.co.uk

In Loving Memory of my
Beloved Dogs xxx

Previously in Book One

Part One ... The Mystic Mirror
And
Part Two ... Fright-Night

After being taunted by Dog Men in the dungeons, the gossips' fate was sealed. Surrain received a letter from Prince Tal, and gave Dayar her reply. Dayar borrowed Surrain's wand and the trio amused themselves in the derelict town. Nightfall was quickly upon the elves. As they dawdled through the misty wood, their fright-night began. Ghostly forces appeared... Wonda's energy was sapped and the trio were left for dead. The three elves, sprawled out across damp ground, had electricity flickering along their bodies. Dayar, Ryar and L.J. recovered, but the only way home was in a rickety boat. The old crones flew above the elves, demanding the letter addressed to Prince Tal. After a frightful struggle, the elves finally made it to Magentis Castle. Dayar placed Surrain's letter on the message table... In the eerie darkness, the youngsters had more spine-chilling moments; giggles were heard coming from behind the wavering curtains. The terrified trio pelted downstairs, only to be confronted by the guards on duty. After a lengthy chat, the elves returned home...

Introduction

A star of wonder shining bright,
High in the sky, it's the northern light.
What lies below? Is it solid or stone?
Who is brave? Venturing into the unknown...

A friend from Drakohsia, with The Game arrives,
The Ring of Fairies five plus five.
Out in the open, revelations unfold,
Stories are heard as the truth be told.

A scheming mortal with a conspiracy in mind,
Is a two-faced demon of a certain kind.
Devising a plot, hatching treason, intrigue,
He's planning an onslaught, a scheme up his sleeve.

While Dog Men are laughing, playing their jokes,
Elsewhere in the land, somebody chokes.
A little bit extra has crawled into the heap,
Hallucinations galore, it sure isn't sleep.

Apparitions appear out of the blue,
Confusion arises, at what to do.
An anti-dote is needed, but is it too late?
Forever Land is near... is this their fate?

The Grim Reaper awaits sitting astride his horse,
Who's displaying a black plume, they're a formidable force.
Forsaken by one, and with so much to fear,
Great power is needed... contact your seer.

A competent wizard, well known by name,
A necessary ritual, to release such pain...
As he completes his spell in foreign rhyme,
Is the seer too late, or just in time?

A Busy Day for Some

Sian and Feebee were up with the larks. It was their first day working at Magentis Castle and they were both eager to start. The sun shone brightly and the two fairies waved to Goover and Bakrus as they flew over the drawbridge.

There was no evidence a storm had hit the kingdom in the early hours, until Sian and Fee opened the door to the entrance hall. Amongst leaves and other bits of debris, shattered glass from the paperweight was scattered around.

Sian glanced at Feebee and tutted. 'Oh look at this mess.' Then she rubbed her arms. 'Ooh can you feel that chill?'

Feebee laughed. 'Mm... Maybe there's a ghost or two lurking about.'

Sian quivered. 'No, it's a cold draft blowing down those stairs, and it's giving me the shivers.'

'Never mind about that, do you fancy tackling this chaos?' asked Fee.

'Yeah no problem,' replied Sian. The fairy pointed her finger at the splattered paperweight and whispered, 'Broosho, glassio, origini, whoosh.' The glass swept round the floor and stairs like sparkling stars. The shiny brittle pieces began to fuse together and in no time at all the paperweight had formed. Sian picked up the small heavy object and said, 'This must belong upstairs.'

The two fairies flew up the wide staircase and found the message table on its side. Fee positioned the three-legged table in the corner and Sian placed the paperweight on top.

Suddenly, the long red curtains began to sway and Sian cried out, 'Come out, come out whoever you are.'

Feebee stepped back and her eyes widened as she gasped, 'That's not funny! I'm already jumpy.'

Sian tutted and said, 'Oh don't be soft. You started it earlier with your wisecracks.' Then Sian flew along the hallway and opened the drapes. 'Huh, there's your answer Fee, a broken window. I'll sort this out, while you fly round the dining room and do a quick tidy up.'

Feebee stood upright with her hands on her hips and scowled at Sian. 'Who made you the boss?'

'Ooh stop being so touchy. You know me, Fee... I like to get things done. Anyway, we don't have to clean the library or go beyond that room, so how about it?'

'All right... But what about preparing the food? Should we take it in turns?'

Sian was on her knees prodding the carpet and she glanced at Feebee. 'No. When it comes to meal-time two heads are better than one. Hey, Fee, this side of Magentis Castle took the brunt of last night's storm. The carpet beneath this window is soaked. I wonder if the wind caused the message table to blow over.'

Feebee disagreed. 'I can't see that happening, the table is too heavy. Think about it for a moment. There's got to be another explanation.'

The fairies dismissed their thoughts and flew round, getting on with their work. Bit by bit, Sian and Feebee fulfilled their duties, but neither of them came across Surrain's letter addressed to Prince Tal.

Meanwhile, Surrain had just arrived home after taking Veela and Sovran out for a run. The little fairy made a pot of dandelion tea and sat at her kitchen table, re-reading the letter she'd received from Prince Tal. Surrain looked forward to her party later that day and whiled away the morning.

By the time Prince Tal arose, Sian and Fee had completed their chores. The Prince left his chambers and walked towards the message table. He expected to find a letter from Surrain, but to his dismay, the message table was empty. Prince Tal sighed with disappointment. Nevertheless, he proceeded downstairs to ensure preparations were in place for meal-time. The Prince was pleasantly surprised by Sian and Feebee's work; more so in the kitchen, which was exceptionally clean and tidy. All was well, so Prince Tal retired to his room to complete some unfinished paperwork.

Dayar, Ryar and L.J. had already called at Magentis Castle to collect their messages. There was nothing on the table, so they took it for granted Prince Tal had received Surrain's letter. Now the youngsters had time on their hands and decided to return Wonda, the little fairy's wand. The elves took their football and played in the woods, whilst making their way to Surrain's.

Dayar, Ryar and L.J. soon arrived at the little fairy's cottage. Dayar knocked on the door and after a few seconds they heard the latch being lifted.

Surrain appeared with a smile on her face. 'Hello there. I must say, you three look quite flustered.'

L.J. picked up the football and said, 'We've being playing ouw favouwite game.' Then he lifted his foot. 'Look at ouw new boots off Wonda. These awe gweat fow kicking the ball, but we get weally hot.'

Surrain laughed. 'I bet you do,' she replied. 'Make yourselves comfortable in the garden, and I'll join you shortly with some refreshments.' A few moments later, Surrain returned with a tray of almond slices, carrot cake, three rosy apples and fresh orange juice.

The little fairy placed the tray on a small table and sat on a mushroom seat. 'Here you are,' she said...'Tuck in before meal-time.'

Anything to do with sweet food put a smile on the elves' faces. 'Thank you,' they said simultaneously.

'You're welcome.' Then Surrain noticed Ryar inspecting his cake. 'What's the matter, Ryar?'

The young elf looked at Surrain and said, 'The other day I heard the grown-ups talking. They mentioned hydra-dragonated fat and said it's mixed into cakes and food. Is there any h-d fat in this cake?'

Surrain shook her head and replied, 'Certainly not. There's never been a need for us fairies to use such a distasteful product... that's a mortal way. I'll just give you a brief explanation... The humans used to mix hydra-dragonated fat into their food for many years. After some time, dragons and the hydra (seven-headed-serpents) were rarely seen. But that didn't stop mortals from experimenting. As well as using vegetable oil, they turned to their livestock for the oily substance, and this mixed with other ingredients, turned into hydrogenated fat.' Surrain shuddered and uttered, 'Hydrogenated fat is no good for anyone... it clogs the arteries. Anyway, Ryar, I hope that's put your mind at ease and answered your question.'

The youngster smiled and said, 'Yes thanks, it has.'

Surrain glanced at Dayar. 'By the way, have I any messages?'

Dayar raised his eyebrows and shook his head. 'No, not today... We've come to return your wand and to thank you for lending Wonda to us.'

Surrain leant towards the youngsters and whispered, 'Did you cast many spells?'

The two young elves began to giggle, but Dayar kept a straight face and replied, 'No not really. When I did ask Wonda to perform a spell, she was brill!'

'Well, everything seems to be in order, so I won't ask any questions. Listen, I'm having a party this afternoon in true faerie style. Do you want to join me and the other fairies by the waterfall at 2pm?'

Dayar sniggered and replied, 'No, it's a girlie afternoon.' At that very moment Ryar and L.J. sighed. When Dayar heard them and looked at their miserable faces, he also sighed. Then he tutted and said, 'All right... Surrain, thanks for the invitation, we will come to your party.' Dayar glanced at Ryar and L.J. muttering, 'I can't be doing with looking at your sulky faces all day.'

Ryar and L.J. were so pleased with Dayar's change of heart they nudged each other, punched the air and cried out 'Y-e-s!'

Dayar exhaled and said, 'Hey you two... don't get too excited.' Seconds later Dayar turned to Surrain. 'We'll be off now. See you later.'

The little fairy waved goodbye to the munching trio as they made their way down her path. Surrain was about to recite a spell, so Wonda would respond to her commands, when she heard Dayar shouting her name.

'Surrain, Surrain!'

As the little fairy opened her door, she was quite concerned to find Dayar standing there, looking very anxious. 'Goodness me, Dayar... Are you all right?'

'Yes,' he quietly replied. 'It's just...erm...can I use Wonda one more time?'

Surrain shook her head, 'Ooh, is that all? I thought you were upset. Here you are,' she said, handing the tiny wand across. 'I'll leave you to it and nip indoors. Just call me when you're ready.'

'Thanks Surrain.' Dayar held the wand in his hand and whispered, 'Wonda. I want to ask you a couple of questions.'

Wonda's face appeared looking tired and drawn. 'Hello, Dayar. How can I help you?' she asked wearily.

Dayar's smiling expression soon changed. 'Ooh, you don't look too good. I'm not sure now.'

'I'm fine, Dayar. I only need to rest. And I'm more than capable of performing a spell. Go on, ask me anything.'

Dayar sighed. 'Well, remember the oars that turned into magic brooms and chased the old crones? What's happened to them and the boat?'

Wonda smiled. 'There's no need to worry, Dayar. Ibsis and Igfreid were only harassed by the brooms for a little while. Then everything returned to its rightful place. Do you want to know anything else?'

'No thanks, Wonda. I know you're exhausted due to our foolish behaviour yesterday. And I hope you have a quick recovery. Before you go, I just want to say you're a little genius.'

Dayar called out to Surrain and handed her the wand. 'Thanks...see you later.'

Dayar joined Ryar and L.J. who were waiting by the garden gate. The trio continued to play football, and before long they arrived on home turf.

Tekwah's Star

After meal-time, Dayar, Ryar and L.J. returned to the woods. The elves looked forward to Surrain's party and tree-hopped near the waterfall.

The time was approaching 2pm. Nomi, Laurel and Bracken, along with their animals, had already arrived in the dell and sat on the grass yattering. Within moments, the three fairies were joined by their companions, Tamzin, Taneesha, Sian, Fee and Jessica. The fairies sat in a circle and giggled with excitement as they waited for Surrain.

Jessica was the only tomboy fairy amongst her friends. She was petite and pretty, with long blonde hair. Jessica didn't have a dress to her name; each day she wore a different coloured blouse with the sleeves rolled up to her elbows, blue dungarees and ankle boots. Earlier that day, Jessica had visited Drakohsia and returned with another one of their companions, a Draemid fairy called Taz.

Most of the inhabitants living in Drakohsia are Tekwah's People of the Draemid Nation. They are a telepathic community having...

<u>D</u>irect <u>R</u>eading <u>A</u>bility <u>E</u>ntering <u>M</u>inds <u>I</u>ncluding <u>D</u>reams.

At the most northerly point in the Kingdom of Deyn is Tekwah's Star...the North Star... the brightest. Directly below lies a cave which is no ordinary rock formation. Within this cavern, two passages lead to alien land; one being Drakohsia, the other Gargolia, a land inhabited by winged gargoyles and other weird creatures. A strong whirling current of air is present inside the cave and this is known as the vortex. The power of the vortex, which has a spiralling motion, draws anyone and anything into its path; they are engulfed and pulled into the whirlwind, tumbling out of the other side. The passage leading to Drakohsia is directly ahead, whereas the path to Gargolia is to the far right of the cave. Occasionally, the Kingdom of Deyn is shaken by a tremor, and this causes the entrance to the cave to seal up at both ends. When this strange phenomenon takes place, those visiting the other side are trapped in that land. It can take days or weeks for the cave mouth to reveal itself again, although it has been known to take years. Due to the danger, only Surrain and Jessica are brave enough to endure this perilous journey.

The ring of fairies decided to settle in an open area, a few metres from the water's edge. Suddenly, Becky, Orfeo and Reah jumped up. The dogs ran towards Veela and Sovran.

Meanwhile, Surrain, who was in a world of her own, flew down and landed beside her friends. 'Hi everyone... Wow, this is a good turnout!'

Nomi was excited and couldn't hold back any longer. 'Surrain, look towards the waterfall.'

All heads turned. The water cascaded into the whirlpool below and, as the sun's rays caught the spray, three brightly coloured rainbows formed.

Then, on a ledge to the right of the falls, a fairy appeared with open arms. 'Ta da!'

This dainty fairy, called Taz, flicked back her shoulder length brown hair and gazed at the group with her light-green eyes. Taz was known as Faerie of Dance. She twirled around in her blue sparkly jeans and black zip-up jacket. Taz clicked her fingers and her faithful friend, an Alsatian named Shadow, appeared by her side. Before any of the fairies had time to speak, Taz and Shadow vanished. Seconds later, Taz and her dog materialized near the group.

Taz had a beaming smile and knelt beside Surrain. 'Long time no see.'

'Yeah, what a surprise, a ten-star reunion at last,' replied Surrain. 'How are you and Shadow?'

Taz glanced at her dog as he joined the other canines. 'We're great! I feel all the better for seeing you and this bunch of good-for-nothings.' As the fairies laughed, Taz added, 'Guess what I've got?'

Surrain's curiosity was roused. She raised her eyebrows and cried out, 'Is it the game? Have you brought Tekwah's Star?'

'What else?' replied Taz. Suddenly the boxed game appeared in the centre of the circle. 'We'll have a good ol' yatter and catch up. Then we'll play Tekwah's Star.'

Surrain looked across at Jessica. 'Thanks for taking the chance and going to Drakohsia... I owe you one.'

'You're welcome,' replied Jessica. She brushed back her long golden locks. 'This is a special occasion Surrain. I couldn't let you down. Now let's get the party going with an interesting topic. Have you any ideas?'

Tamzin wiggled her finger in the air. 'I always find the story about Prince Tal fascinating.' She tilted her head and sighed. 'It's so... so romantic.'

The fairies muttered and looked at each other with somewhat strange expressions.

Laurel shook her head. 'Romantic? You've lost the plot! The Prince was a toddler, alone in an alien world. Where's the romance in that?'

Then Nomi cried out, 'Let's not bicker. Surrain, Jessica or Taz can choose one of these stories... The Drakohsian Nubble-Thrup Imps, How Tekwah's Star Came About, or, The Chronicles of Prince Tal... you know, an early account of the Prince's history. So, which is it to be?'

The fairies giggled and Surrain laughed aloud. 'I like that,' cried the little fairy, 'The Chronicles of Prince Tal.'

Taz clapped her hands to get attention. 'I'll be the storyteller. Trouble is I have to be home before nightfall. But I have time for two stories and a dance. I'll start with Tekwah's Star. When I've finished, I'll tell you about Prince Tal... my version. The Nubble-Thrup Imps can wait. I'll just say, they have distinct physical characteristics... they're all tiny, plump and clumsier than elves.'

A few twigs snapped and the fairies turned their heads. They saw the elf messengers sitting in a tree behind them, and a chuckle rippled through the small gathering.

Then Bracken stretched her arms in the air and yawned. 'So, Taz... You're going to refresh our memories with these fascinating tales, eh?'

Laurel tutted. 'You know, Bracken, you can be a right so and so at times! We enjoy stories.'

'I couldn't agree more,' added Taneesha.

Nomi rose to her feet. 'Ooh, bickering again. I suggest we 'collect'... then we can sit comfortably and listen to Taz while we munch.'

'Sounds good to me,' said Surrain.

Jessica sighed. 'But the game... when are we going to play Tekwah's Star?' she asked anxiously.

Taz laughed. 'Don't worry, Jess. After all your efforts, I'll make time. The stories will be short and sweet.'

The fairies flew round the shaded wood and picked special button mushrooms.

Meanwhile, Dayar, Ryar and L.J. sat in a treetop giggling.

It wasn't long before a heap of edible fungi had been gathered, so Taneesha whispered a few magic words. The mushroom mound rose up, and moved through the air, descending inside the circle. Moments later, the fairies returned to their spot and began to feast on their delights.

'Right,' said Taz, and she glanced round the circle. 'I'm going to begin... The Heavenly ten-pointed star is the brightest light in the sky. My people named it Tekwah's Star, as tekwahs means ten and ten is our special number. Tekwah's Star can be seen distinctly in Drakohsia, and this marvel illuminates most of the southern region. Directly below this celestial body are the Teogotha Hills and the entrance to the cave with the vortex, windy hollow. The view of the star is quite different here, in the Kingdom of Deyn. Although the same star shines brightly in your sky, it's so far away the ten points are a blur. The celestial body is your North Star, but we fairies call it Tekwah's Star. A mountainous region called North Point lies below this twinkling light, and this is the area where the cave with the vortex can be found. This cave is the only link, the only connection to our worlds. Surrain came across the cave by accident, when the power of the whirlwind drew her in. Surrain entered my world, Drakohsia. We met and have been friends ever since. I followed Surrain back into your kingdom and we visited each other regularly, until the rock face sealed and the entrance on both sides vanished. As soon as the entrance revealed itself, our travels resumed. We both know the cave mouth could seal at any time, usually after an earth tremor, so now we are wary of this rare phenomenon.' Taz paused for a few seconds; she ate a mushroom, took a sip of her drink and continued with the story. 'Surrain and I were full of ideas. One sunny afternoon, we decided to create a board game. We flew round the Kingdom of Deyn, taking in the sights. Then we drew a rough map of the area. Surrain and I designed the game on a chequered board and called it Tekwah's Star. The name seemed quite appropriate, but it was more symbolic, as the ten glowing points of the star represent each one of us...'

All of a sudden Surrain began to cough. Then, as she grasped her neck, she began to choke on a large piece of fungus lodged in her throat.

Without any hesitation, Nomi reached across and banged Surrain across her back. 'Are you all right?' she cried out.

Surrain massaged the front of her neck and gulped. Then she replied, 'I am now. Thanks, Nomi.'

Taz squinted whilst staring at her friend. 'Surrain, do you want me to carry on with my next story?'

'Yeah, of course I do. But don't make it too long.'

Tamzin groaned. 'Ooh, you'll be missing loads out.'

Taz replied, 'Stop moaning, Tamzin. After I've told the story, we'll play the game. Then we'll dance and the elf messengers can join us.' Taz purposely raised her voice so the three elves could hear. 'Now don't forget, the mortal population must never ever find out what I'm about to tell you. Here goes... Years ago Meidi was in the mountainous region North Point. He was probably exploring the area when he came across the diamond and gold mines. Anyway, he noticed a toddler wandering amongst the rocks. Meidi looked around for an adult, but there wasn't another soul in sight. Due to this, he felt morally obliged to take the boy back to Magentis Castle. The mortals who lived in the castle didn't question Meidi. In fact they assumed the child was a mortal, related to Meidi. They never imagined him to be a Draemid with mind-reading ability. Due to travelling through the vortex at such a tender age, the boy lost most of his power. Nevertheless, Meidi knew he was different. The youngster wore a charm, a ten-pointed star amulet, with Tal etched on the back. But Meidi took the pendant and hid it. After some years, Meidi gave the boy a coveted title, Prince Tal, and he would inherit the Kingdom of Deyn. The Prince lived through his teenage years without question or incident. He was well liked and fitted in perfectly with Meidi's plans. Then a black-haired stranger arrived at Magentis Castle. This person demanded to speak to the ruler of the kingdom. Greega knew something was amiss. The Dog Guard sensed this man's need for answers, a man who looked like Prince Tal, but more advanced in years. Greega immediately escorted the stranger to Meidi's quarters and waited anxiously outside. Meidi sat behind his desk and was visibly shaken by the presence of this stranger. He knew exactly why this man was in his chambers. The dreaded day of truth was finally upon him. Meidi was tense. Afraid of losing the boy he'd brought up to rule his kingdom. Nevertheless, he asked the man to sit down and explain his business. "My name is Tithe," said the stranger. "I am from Drakohsia, a distant land, and I belong to the Tekwah's People of the Draemid Nation. I have waited so long for this day to be upon us, for a chance to be drawn into the whirling turbulence and fall into your kingdom. Many years ago, a child from my nation wandered into forbidden territory. He entered a cave known as windy hollow. Moments later, the boy disappeared as the whirlwind swallowed him up. My people were about to follow the youngster, but the rescue attempt failed; a tremor shook the land and the cave mouth sealed. Recently, an earth tremor shook Teogotha Hills. Somehow this activity affected the entrance to windy hollow, which became visible again. Now I am here seeking answers. Has the waiting paid off? Pray tell me the boy was found and is safe to this day." Meidi told Tithe what he wanted to hear, but the man was still unsure. Tithe asked Meidi if he had any proof of the boy's identity. The Grand Master opened the middle drawer of his desk, taking out the chain and star amulet. As Meidi dropped the piece of jewellery into the cupped hands of Tithe, he noticed the amulet was identical to the one Tithe was wearing over his cloak. Once Tithe had the ten-pointed star in his possession, he sat back and gazed into it intensely. A visible sign of sadness engulfed him. After a few moments of silence, Tithe uttered, "Mm. There's no doubt about it. This amulet belonged to the boy." Tithe leaned over the Grand Master's desk making him feel extremely uncomfortable. "Look at this," said Tithe, showing Meidi the amulet. "There's a dot next to the inscription of Tal's name. When pressed three times, the back of the amulet springs open. This cavity holds a lock of the child's hair. And here it is." Meidi was impressed. "Well I've had the amulet in my possession for many years and never knew that existed."

Tithe sat down and glared at Meidi. "You were not to know what lay behind the beauty of Tekwah's Star," he replied. Tithe told Meidi about the wonder of the star, and how each child is given a precious amulet at birth. When Tithe finished explaining, he sat in silence waiting for a reaction from the Grand Master. Meidi felt uneasy and called out to the Dog Guard, "Greega!" The guard opened the door and found Meidi red-faced and nervous. "Find Prince Tal and escort him to my quarters," he cried. When Greega departed, Tithe tried to reassure Meidi. The Draemid said there would be no problem if Tal wished to stay in this kingdom, as long as he knew where his roots lay... Then Greega returned with the Prince. Tithe stood up. The likeness was unbelievable and Meidi's jaw dropped open. Prince Tal and Tithe were the same height; both had straight black shoulder length hair and a moustache. The only difference was their clothes. Prince Tal wore riding attire, whereas Tithe wore a long dark cloak that swept about his person. Upon meeting, the two men smiled. Then Tithe used telepathy. Prince Tal was totally at ease and capable of understanding. "Yes, Sir," he replied. "And I feel honoured to be in your presence." Deadly silence descended. The two Draemids stood face to face and conversed using telepathy. After some time, Tithe laughed aloud. By now Meidi was extremely anxious, more so when the man glared at him. Tithe thanked Meidi for his hospitality. He then placed both hands on Prince Tal's shoulders. Tithe's eyes welled up and he embraced the Prince. "My dear boy, I am so pleased to have found you. Now I must bid you farewell. But mark my words, I will return." A moment later the Draemid left the room and kingdom. Meidi was clearly unnerved by the whole incident and doubted Prince Tal for the first time. He said, "Have you always been telepathic and kept it a closely guarded secret?" Prince Tal laughed, "No not at all," he replied. The Prince told Meidi he'd just discovered this power, which came as some surprise to him. Then the Prince said he would never leave the kingdom, although he might visit Drakohsia. Meidi's uncertainty lifted and he was somewhat relieved by Prince Tal's answer. Meidi passed the chain and amulet over to Tal and said, "This belongs to you. Wear it for protection against evil forces." Then Meidi pointed out the secret opening. "This container holds a tiny piece of your hair, and it's ideal for magic dust. Now you are old enough to take responsibility and represent me in the outside world. Use the dust wisely." That's it...' Taz sighed. 'The years have flown by and here we are in the present day.'

Questions and Answers

Taz finished storytelling, but the fairies wanted answers.

Tamzin was the most inquisitive and asked the first question, 'Taz, where's your star amulet?'

Taz reached up to her neck and wiggled the charm under Tamzin's nose.

Tamzin still wasn't satisfied. 'Those stories were quite detailed. How come you're so knowledgeable?'

Taz smirked. 'I'm a Draemid.' She chuckled. 'Besides, everyone in Drakohsia is aware of those tales. When Tithe met Prince Tal it was only a few years ago. And Tekwah's Star is legendary.'

'Is it true that Tithe is Prince Tal's father?' asked Fee.

Taz didn't reply... she smiled.

After a short silence Nomi sighed. She frowned and asked a question. 'Taz, there are no mortals living in Drakohsia. Why?'

'Come on, Nomi! You know Draemids can't tolerate the human race. Anyway, we've got the Nubble-Thrup Imps instead. They don't look like typical mortals, but hey, we're all different.'

'Why are they called Nubble-Thrup's?' asked Sian.

'Simple,' replied Taz. 'They're as tall as a nubble and wide as a thrup.'

'Yeah, they look like munchkins!' giggled Surrain.

Everyone roared with laughter.

Then Laurel asked a question. 'How come Draemids can't read our minds?'

'I have no idea. For some reason, telepathy doesn't work on fairies and elves in this kingdom. But as you know, it's different with Draemids.'

'So you know exactly what Prince Tal is thinking?' asked Taneesha.

Taz smiled in a way that riled Surrain, and she replied, 'I certainly do.'

Surrain's expression changed and she scowled at Taz. 'Draemids can block their thoughts. I do know that.'

'Only Draemids brought up in Drakohsia,' said Taz. 'If we need to, we switch off. That prevents telepathy from taking place. But when we're socializing, to switch off is frowned upon.'

'Something has always puzzled me,' uttered Bracken. 'You know the cave called windy hollow? If it's in forbidden territory, why are you allowed to go into that area?'

'Huh. You're interested now, aren't you?' cried Feebee.

Taz reached for another mushroom and glanced at Fee. 'Hey, don't get uptight... we're all in this together. Anyway, Bracken, the answer to your question is easy... the authorities don't know.'

Taneesha suddenly surprised everyone by asking an intelligent question. 'Taz, Tekwah's Star has ten points... most Draemids have family members amounting to ten... Tithe means one-tenth... and I believe the Teogotha Hills has ten mounds. Ten and T seem to be a trait with you Draemids, why?'

'Well, in Drakohsia, ten is a symbol, an exceptional number. Besides being a numeral denoting ten units, it's also a letter. When the number 10 is turned on its side with the one horizontally over the nought, this is the beginning of our alphabet. And don't forget, most Draemids have a name which begins with the letter T.'

Jessica sighed deeply. 'Ooh enough is enough. What about playing the game?'

'Ok,' said Taz. 'We'll play Tekwah's Star now.'

Meanwhile, the three elves were bickering in the treetop.

'Hey listen to this,' said Ryar. 'Hubble nubble toil and trouble.'

Ryar and L.J. giggled, but Dayar shouted out, 'Don't be stupid! It's Hubble-bubble toil and trouble.'

'I know!' yelled Ryar. 'I was having a joke. And don't call me stupid. You're stupider than me.'

'Idiot, there's no such word,' said Dayar.

Ryar knew how to annoy his brother and he shouted, 'Yes there is... I know there is, so there!' Then Ryar's tone changed. 'Hey Dayar, do you know anything about the Nubble-Thrup Imps?'

'I remember Surrain telling me the imps live underground in the north east of Drakohsia.'

'And did Suwwain tell you what they look like?' asked L.J.

'No, it was Taz who described them to me. She said they're short and squat, with big ears and nothing much in between. A bit like you two.'

L.J. tutted and replied, 'Idiot.'

'Yeah, get lost, Dayar, you drimp,' cried Ryar. 'We're not squat and we haven't got big ears either!'

'You will 'ave when I've finished with you!' cried Dayar. Then the youngster reached across and pulled Ryar and L.J. by their ears. A scuffle broke out as the elves threw punches at each other. During the fight broken twigs and leaves fell to the ground. The chaos disturbed the animals resting beneath the tree. Veela, Sovran, Orfeo and Shadow moved behind a clump of bushes, while Becky and Reah sprawled out in the sun. Suddenly, a loud groan of disapproval came from within the tree and its branches began to shake. Misty was oblivious to the goings on and woke up after a falling twig cracked him across his head. The cat lost his balance and wailed with pain as he struck a number of branches on the way down. Luckily for him, Misty landed on all fours and dashed towards Laurel. Misty flew into Laurel's arms and she cradled her cat, making him feel secure.

Meanwhile, the tree continued to wave its branches, trying to dislodge Dayar, Ryar and L.J. The fairies were accustomed to the elves being around, nevertheless heads turned at the noisy outburst. The thick arm-like limbs of the tree shook vigorously. Then everyone heard two loud thuds. Seconds later, the fairies watched Ryar and L.J. clamber to their feet.

Nomi giggled and shouted, 'Have you been listening to all our secrets?'

Ryar was taken aback by Nomi's remark and cried out, 'What do you mean? You know whatever we hear is never repeated.'

Bracken gave her two-penny-worth. 'Mm, just keep it that way.'

Ryar looked a little dismayed. He placed his arm round L.J.'s shoulder and whispered, 'Huh, I always get the blame. Come on L.J. we've got to make a woody apology.' The two youngsters looked up the tree and Ryar beckoned his brother. 'Come on, Dayar. The tree is really annoyed. You know what we've got to do now.'

Dayar swung down and the three elves proceeded. They placed their hands against the tree trunk and Dayar began to apologize.

'Sorry for being disrespectful. No offence intended. As I am the eldest, my actions were well out of order. Please accept an apology. I will behave in the future.'

'Me too,' uttered Ryar.

'And me,' cried L.J. 'Pwomise we'll be good.'

When the remorseful elves moved their hands away from the tree, they heard a deep rumbling sound. The tree shuddered and suddenly a number of bulging eyes emerged from nodules covering the trunk. Then, a wide mouth appeared on the lower part of the tree. A deep hoarse voice uttered, 'I will not tolerate this unruly behaviour. In the future, if you want to conduct yourselves in such a manner, go elsewhere. There's a whole kingdom for you to go wild and act like savages. I do accept your apology. But if there's any more skirmishing up my tree, I won't be responsible for my actions. You may go now.'

Dayar, Ryar and L.J. stepped back. The tree closed his eyes and, once again, small rounded nodules were revealed.

During this time, the ring of fairies finished playing Tekwah's Star.

'That was the shortest game ever,' yelled Sian.

Nomi laughed. She waved her hands in the air and cried out, 'Hey hey and I'm the winner!'

Taz rose to her feet and said, 'Time to dance.'

Surrain looked up and around. The little fairy beckoned Dayar, Ryar and L.J. 'Come on you three!'

The elves didn't waste any time. After their ticking off, they wanted to enjoy the rest of the afternoon. Dayar, Ryar and L.J. moved their shoulders and wiggled their hips as they made their way towards the fairies. Giggles rippled through the small gathering and, with a fluttering of wings, the dancing began. The fairies bobbed up, down, round and around, and sang until they were exhausted.

An hour or so before dusk, Taz sighed and called Shadow. 'Come on boy, we'd better make a move.'

While the fairies said their goodbyes, Dayar, Ryar and L.J. slipped away. The elves tree-hopped and moved deeper into the woods.

Taz handed Jessica the game. 'Keep it with you,' she said. Then Taz walked towards Surrain. 'I've had a wonderful afternoon. I'm really pleased for you, Surrain, and I wish you both all the best. Try and let me know when you've set a date for your wedding.'

The two fairies smiled and embraced each other. Suddenly Taz changed her expression, indicating alarm. A warning about Meidi came to the forefront of her mind. There was something else... bad intention and pain. But it was all so vague. Taz was confused. She didn't know whether this feeling was aimed at Surrain or Prince Tal, or both of them. 'I must warn Surrain,' she muttered.

'What did you say, Taz?' asked the little fairy.

Taz didn't have a chance to tell Surrain. She was distracted by the fairies wishing her farewell.

Becky and Reah wandered towards Shadow. He looked delightfully content and wagged his tail. Then Shadow whispered sweet nothings in Becky and Reah's ears.

'It's time to depart and head for the vortex,' cried Taz.

'Have a safe journey,' replied the fairies.

Taz smiled and said, 'Fingers crossed.' Then Taz held onto Shadow and they both vanished.

The Soul Collectors

Moments after Taz and Shadow departed, Jessica placed the game on the grass. Excitement filled the air, but the mood slowly changed as evil forces approached the area.

Dayar, Ryar and L.J. were frightened by dark shadows and decided to tree hop back to the group. Meanwhile, eight fairies were engrossed in the party atmosphere, while Surrain appeared to be in a world of her own. The little fairy wandered off, but no-one noticed; nor did these elusive beings realise, a group of sinister entities loomed under the nearby trees.

The elves sat high up on a wide branch and watched the giggling fairies return to their places.

Jessica was itching to continue with the board game and said, 'Let's play Tekwah's Star again.'

'That's not a bad idea,' said Laurel. 'There's still sometime before darkness falls.'

Just as the fairies nodded in agreement, Dayar shouted from the treetop, 'Can we play too?'

'Yeah, come on,' replied Nomi. 'Be quick and choose a partner.'

The giddy trio slid down the tree and raced across the grass. Dayar picked Laurel as a partner and sat beside her. Then Ryar chose Nomi and squeezed in. L.J. wanted Surrain as a partner, but he knew that was impossible. He had seen Surrain heading for the woods sometime ago.

L.J. sighed. 'I'm not playing. I'll just watch.'

'You can be my partner,' said Jessica. Then she flew towards L.J. and cuddled him.

'Ooh I can't bweathe,' gasped the youngster, as he tried to push Jessica off. 'All wight, I'll play the game if you stop squashing me!'

Jessica kissed L.J.'s rosy cheek and the game began.

Within moments of starting Tekwah's Star, a cold chill swept round the small gathering.

Laurel rubbed her arms and looked about. 'Ooh a shiver just ran down my spine.'

Nomi quivered and replied, 'Mm, me too.'

Sian shuddered and glanced into the sky. 'The sun's shining brightly, but that chill is ever so eerie.'

Bracken sighed. 'It is a ghostly atmosphere...even the birds have stopped singing.'

Feebee pushed Bracken and said, 'Don't be scaring the elves, not in the middle of the woods.' Then Fee looked into the near distance towards the trees. 'I must admit, there is a depressing influence over there.'

Jessica sighed. 'Oh great, everyone's lost interest in the game now.'

Dayar blurted out, 'Hey don't be like that. We'll play.' He glanced at Ryar and L.J.

The frowning youngsters didn't reply. They sat tight-lipped and stared wide-eyed at Dayar.

Tamzin fluttered her wings. 'Ooh, I've had enough of this. I'm going home. Come on Taneesha.'

Sian nudged Fee and said, 'Yeah, it's time we went home too.'

The four fairies didn't waste any time. They said farewell to their friends and left the party, unaware of Surrain's absence.

As Jessica packed away the game, she said, 'I don't like this chill, it feels quite unpleasant. But we've had a lovely afternoon.' Then Jessica frowned and cried out, 'Where's Surrain?'

'Surrain went for a walk ages ago,' replied Dayar.

'What? On her own?' asked Nomi.

Dayar shook his head. 'No, Surrain had company. Becky and Reah walked on either side of her.'

'That's strange,' uttered Nomi. 'Becky and Reah have never done anything like that before.'

'Now you come to mention it, something did seem a bit odd,' said Dayar. 'Surrain kept turning her head to the right and left, as if she was looking for someone.'

'Yeah, I remember that,' cried Ryar.

'I do too,' added L.J. Then the young elf shouted, 'What if someone was following Suwwain?'

L.J.'s comment unnerved the anxious group even more.

'We're all worried now,' said Bracken. The plum-haired fairy flew into the air and looked towards the shrubbery. 'I can see Veela,

Sovran and Orfeo. They're sleeping under a clump of ferns.' Bracken sighed. 'Listen, I'm going to look for Surrain and the two dogs. You lot stay here and wait for us to return. Hopefully I won't be long.' Bracken vanished and everyone sat on the grass yattering.

No sooner had Bracken left, when the three fairies and elves turned their heads at the sound of a galloping horse. The ground pounded and several dark shadows moved swiftly overhead. Hoof prints sank deep into the earth and a loud neighing of the ghostly horse rang in the group's ears. As the waft of a great beast raced by, a black plume fluttered down and landed inside the circle. The elves were struck with fear. The trio jumped to their feet and looked around warily. Misty sprang up from Laurel's arms, fur standing on end. Meanwhile, Veela, Sovran and Orfeo woke up with a start. The frightened animals pelted towards the fairies.

Laurel, Nomi and Jessica knew there was only one creature capable of making such a terrifying sound.

Nomi grabbed L.J. 'It's all right. You're safe with us,' she cried.

Laurel seemed agitated. She glanced at the elves and said, 'Calm down and stop worrying. I've just uttered a protection spell.'

'What?' yelled Ryar, 'why do we need a protection spell?'

Laurel sighed and replied, 'To keep us safe. We're out of harms way now, sheltered by an invisible dome.'

Veela was uneasy. She looked round anxiously and cried out, 'Surrain! Oh where's Surrain?'

Then Orfeo noticed his sister was missing. 'Where's Becky?'

'Reah and Bracken are missing too,' shouted Sovran.

Jessica reached out to the fretful animals. 'Don't be alarmed. Just settle down. They'll be back shortly.'

The trees in the near distance stirred. As their branches moved to and fro, a dark cloud hovered above them.

L.J. sat quivering. The pale-faced youngster bent his knees up to his chin and wrapped his hands over his head, muttering to himself.

Ryar said, 'I can't hear you L.J. Speak up.'

The little elf raised his head and peered through his fingers. In a trembling voice he replied, 'Why is this happening? I want Suwwain.'

Laurel couldn't take much more. She clenched her teeth and breathed deeply. Her nerves were frayed by the frightened elves and animals. All of a sudden she snapped and shrieked, 'Shut-up! Sit quietly. I've had enough of this palaver, it's getting us nowhere. We're safe in here... OK?!'

There was silence. Then everyone looked fearfully towards the howling trees. They saw the angel of death standing beside his horse. The black steed's silver armour, which covered his head and legs, was dazzling. But to add to their fear, the group saw small black hooded entities, fluttering around the Grim Reaper. Within the blink of an eye, the angel of death mounted his horse and began galloping towards the gathering.

'Look away. Focus on Veela, Sovran and Orfeo!' cried Nomi.

As the black horse cantered round the circle, a mighty cry deafened the fairies and elves.

'Arghhhhhh... Arghhhhhh!' roared the Grim Reaper.

Moments later the dark angel's horse reared up and struck the invisible barrier with his hooves. After that pounding, the Grim Reaper rode away and once again silence descended. During this time, Dayar, Ryar and L.J.'s hearts were throbbing with fear.

Then the fairies, elves and animals gasped. The group watched with horror as ten hooded ghouls flew screeching towards them. Eerie cries echoed all around. Suddenly, the dark hooded creatures crashed against the outside of the barrier, trying to smash their way through.

'The soul collectors are gonna get in. And there's one for each of us!' yelled Dayar.

The small entities circled the dome, striking its surface with all their might.

The animals huddled together, while the fairies sat tight with their arms wrapped around the three elves.

L.J. didn't utter a word, but Ryar stood up and cried out, 'Did you see the Grim Reaper's horse? He's wearing silver battledress.' Then Ryar picked up the black plume, and yelled, 'Look at this! We're dead! We're dead! Ooh we're dead!'

Jessica sighed and tried to reassure the youngster. 'Ryar don't be so dramatic. We won't come to any harm. Like Laurel said, we're completely safe in here.'

But the Grim Reaper knew the score. Once again the thunder of hooves began to pound the ground. The shrieking soul collectors darted into the nearby trees, making way for this terrifying duo. The galloping horse neighed loudly and came to a halt near the invisible dome. The black stallion glared at the group with a menacing look in his eyes. Seconds later, the steed snorted streams of flames from his wide nostrils as he struck his foreleg into the earth.

Meanwhile, the Grim Reaper was in his glory. He roared as he swung a ball and chain high above his head. The dark angel leant forwards, towards the barrier and smashed his weapon across the side...shattering the dome. The steed reared up and neighed like never before. Then the Grim Reaper and his horse disappeared into the shadows.

Familiar Faces

While chaos erupted in the dell, Surrain, who was oblivious to the imminent danger, wandered deeper into the woods.

Becky and Reah could sense evil closing in on them, but they couldn't persuade Surrain to turn back.

The little fairy began to hallucinate and this confused her already clouded mind. As Surrain walked past the trees, she was startled as they burst into life. A multitude of bulging eyes appeared up and down each groaning tree. Then a curling mouth emerged at the base of every tree trunk.

Surrain turned in circles before glancing into the sky. She watched in amazement as four orange rabbits appeared from nowhere and flew happily through the clouds. Then the small mammals stopped in mid-air. Surrain was puzzled by their behaviour and stared at the creatures. The rabbits suddenly changed form. Snarling beasts glared at Surrain with their glowing red eyes. After a while, the little demons nose-dived towards Surrain and she ducked, falling across Becky.

Surrain clambered to her feet, 'Ooh, Sovran, I'm sorry. It was those hideous beings coming at me.'

Becky sighed deeply and said, 'Surrain, there's nothing there. And I'm not Sovran... I'm Becky.'

Surrain's head veered from side to side. As the little fairy looked down at Becky, the cream poodle and white wolf began to blend into one. Surrain glanced to her left. Reah looked up with her big brown eyes, but Surrain saw Veela's image merge into the greyhound. Surrain gasped for air. She lifted her hand to her forehead and fell to her knees.

'What's wrong with me? I feel so dizzy,' she muttered.

Suddenly a squeaking mouse jumped in front of Surrain. The little fairy didn't hear his shrill cries. Instead the mouse had a deep voice, with prolonged low-pitched tones. Surrain couldn't make sense of anything. She stood up, and continued talking to herself as peculiar creatures appeared before her eyes. Pink elephants popped their heads in and out of rabbit holes. Screeching red mushrooms flew by at shoulder height. Wooshie-bough imps soared round the trees and a number of snarling Orpinook congregated by the stream.

Just as Becky walked ahead, a mass of leaves rose up in front of Surrain. The foliage formed into a dark eerie apparition, reaching out to the little fairy. As a light wind blew round the trees, the leaves dispersed and fluttered overhead.

Surrain was thrown into a panic by the flying debris and yelled, 'Veela, Sovran, look out!'

Reah walked beside Surrain and sighed. She raised her head and said, 'There's nothing to fear, Surrain. They're only leaves.'

Surrain didn't hear Reah's words of reassurance. She only heard, 'Cuckoo. You're going cuckoo.' The little fairy was in despair and looked round fearfully. 'Who's there? What do you want?'

Surrain wandered about, trying to flutter her wings. Then the ground shuddered. Stalks of climbing ivy began to curl out of the forest floor. The trailing plants crept across the ground. As the wiggling leaves inched towards Surrain, the stems grew taller and thicker. Surrain was petrified and she crouched beside the nearest tree, covering her eyes. As the green stalks sprang up and out, they groaned and withered. Surrain heard muffled cries and moved her hands away from her face. There was no sign of the climbing ivy and she breathed a sigh of relief. Feeling dazed and in a somewhat delirious state, Surrain leaned back into the tree. Becky and Reah knew Surrain was incoherent, so they sat on either side of her, keeping a watchful eye.

All of a sudden, two arm-like branches reached down and lifted Surrain to her feet. Then a deep voice uttered, 'Come on Faerie of the Forest. Up you get and off you go.'

Becky and Reah were taken by surprise. The two dogs jumped up and growled. Surrain stood back and stared at the tree. He rolled his bulging eyes, raised his eyebrows and grinned like a Cheshire cat.

Becky whispered to Reah. 'Did you see that? I don't like this, there's something weird going on.'

'Huh, so you've just noticed?' replied Reah, sarcastically.

Becky growled at Reah and through gritted teeth she snarled, 'Don't be smart with me.'

Reah was angry and also returned the threat with a snarl. 'I forgot what a grumpy, thin-skinned old sod you are. Can't take sarcasm... Can't take any blame. Any excuse for a bust-up with me. Well, Becky, we're in this together. We've no time for disagreements, not while Surrain is going loopy and not when there's something really sinister out there.'

Becky scanned the area. 'All right... you win this time. Let's get Surrain back to the dell, before we're in real trouble.'

Reah cried out, 'Becky-Bow... hello. We're out here on our own and we're seeing things too.'

While Becky and Reah bickered, a hazy cloud appeared in front of Surrain. The little fairy didn't seem at all bothered and she walked through the mist, calling out to the dogs, 'Come on, you two.'

Surrain, Becky and Reah found themselves on a country lane. Blue and orange hedgerows grew on either side of this narrow path, with pink fields beyond. Surrain continued into the unknown, oblivious to her surroundings. The trio approached a recess, with a gateway leading on to pink fields. Surrain opened a bright-green farm gate and made her way through with Becky and Reah following. They walked across the cherry-coloured fields and down the hill towards a row of trees. Surrain and the two dogs came to a trickling stream. Just across the water, leaning on a tree, stood a tall slim man with his head lowered. The man wore a wide-brimmed hat and a drover's coat. Surrain gazed at him, while Becky and Reah sat quietly by the little fairy's side. The man slowly raised his head. Surrain felt wary and fearful towards this stranger, who looked neither young nor old.

The man took off his hat and smiled at Surrain. 'Hello, fairy doll. I've had a quart of loopigoo, but don't worry, I won't harm you.'

Surrain also smiled, and the man promptly returned his hat covering his mop of fair-hair.

Surrain was baffled. She couldn't make any sense of the situation. 'Are you real?' she asked.

The man sniggered, 'Of course I am!' he exclaimed.

'So I'm not seeing things? Are you some kind of angel?'

The man laughed aloud, 'Fairy doll, do I look like an angel?'

Surrain bit her bottom lip. Then she replied, 'Angels take many forms.'

'True,' he said, 'but I can assure you, I'm a man... angels are neither male nor female.'

Surrain's expression changed and her worried look concerned the stranger.

'Are you all right doll?'

Surrain glanced at the man and replied, 'But Kirrey's my guardian angel and he is male.'

The man shook his head, 'No, no,' he replied. 'Let me enlighten you. Angels are divine messengers, pure, gentle, spiritual beings with no gender.'

Surrain frowned. 'Who are you?'

'I am your sanity.'

The little fairy sighed, 'I've seen you before.'

'I'm sure you have,' he replied.

All of a sudden, the man appeared beside Surrain with two portraits in his hands. 'My forte lies within the arts. I excel in poetry and painting. Feast your eyes upon these portraits. I specialize in painting war scenes.'

Surrain was surprised and said, 'Those pictures are really good. They look as if they were painted during the event itself.'

'They were. I was there amongst the butchery.'

'But those are scenes from battles that took place in the outside world many years ago.'

The paintings vanished and the man replied, 'True. I'm kind of like... like a time traveller.' Then he sniggered and said, 'No I'm not... only kidding.'

Surrain sighed. 'Can't you come straight out with the facts? That comment is annoying, to say the least.'

The sky darkened and it began to rain.

Surrain looked up and breathed deeply. 'Ooh, rain is so clean and fresh.'

The man also raised his head. 'Nature is wonderful.'

Surrain's curiosity was getting to her and she asked another question. 'Who are you really?'

'I told you. I'm your sanity.'

The fairy giggled and said, 'Look at us chatting in the rain. Are you on your way home?'

The man suddenly burst into rhyme... 'I walked through the gate and decided to wait, for a fairy to appear out of the blue... I'm going to the valley of flowers, where I spend many hours, dreaming of dreams come true.'

Surrain took little notice of the rhyme. She just sighed again.

The man lifted his hand and moved it across the little fairy's back. 'Surrain contact the seer Jozeffri, before it's too late.'

With that the man was gone.

Surrain looked around. There was no stream, no pink fields and no rain. The little fairy was standing in the woods, beside a groaning tree.

Becky shuddered. The poodle glanced at Reah wide-eyed and spoke softly, 'Ooh what next?'

Moments later, a multitude of eyes popped out of the nodules covering the tree trunk. Becky and Reah gulped as the bulging eyes gazed at them.

Surrain didn't utter a word. She just stared at Becky and Reah with an expression of uncertainty.

Then Reah turned her head to the right and yelled, 'Becky. Look what's heading our way.'

Surrain was startled by Reah's cry and spun round. 'Oh no,' she gasped.

Three ghostly figures glided towards the trio, and Surrain backed into the groaning tree. All of a sudden, two branches wrapped themselves round Surrain's body.

'Let me go,' cried the struggling little fairy.

The moaning tree sighed, 'It is t-o-o late... t-o-o late.'

Meanwhile, Becky and Reah stood snarling at the misty apparitions. Then a cluster of silver stars showered over the dogs. Although Becky and Reah were mesmerised, captivated by the three spirits, they were still aware of a hostile force that lurked in the forest.

The ghostly figures glided closer to Surrain. When the apparitions were almost upon the little fairy, she saw that their faces were strangely familiar.

Surrain trembled with fear and cried out, 'It's you. What do you want? Why has this tree seized me? And what's happened to my faerie magic? I'm powerless.'

The beautiful young woman, dressed in a flowing cerise gown, raised her hand. Her two male companions took this as a sign and drifted back.

The ghostly fairy's long dark hair swayed in the gentle breeze. She gazed at Surrain with her green eyes and said, 'Even though you are delirious, there is no doubting our identity. And oh... question after question. So Faerie of the Forest, speak our names if you will.'

Surrain continued to struggle. As she turned one way then the other, the twig-like claws gripped her body tightly. Frightened, breathless and weary, the little fairy cried out, 'You are Princess Debs. And you are accompanied by your brothers, Prince Daheyl and Prince Deyn. Tell me... what have I done to deserve this? Why am I being held against my will?'

Princess Debs sighed deeply. Her brothers had grim expressions and slowly shook their heads. Prince Deyn stared at Surrain with his smouldering brown eyes, while Prince Daheyl's piercing blue eyes penetrated Surrain's being.

Then Princess Debs spoke softly and replied, 'Surrain, your mind is playing tricks... wandering in a curious manner. You are confused and have no control whatsoever.'

Surrain demanded an answer. 'What do you mean? Tell me! What do you want?'

Princess Debs sighed again, 'Dear little fairy. You are scourged with blight. S-c-o-u-r-g-e-d with blight... Do Not drink. Do Not let water pass your lips. If days do pass, it will be t-o-o late.'

The ghostly figures began to drift back and faded into the shaded forest. They slowly shook their heads, while the haunting sadness in their voices grew ever faint. 'Ooo... it's t-o-o late... t-o-o late, ooo.'

Surrain, still gripped by the branches, felt feeble and weak. She closed her eyes and lowered her head.

After some moments, Surrain felt the ground vibrating beneath her feet. The pounding became stronger. Then the little fairy heard the distant sound of a neighing horse. That vital spark lifted Surrain's spirit and she mumbled, 'I can only hope Prince Tal is approaching.'

As the pounding hooves closed in, Becky and Reah sensed an evil force. Suddenly, a shadow covered Surrain and the two dogs. Becky and Reah moved rapidly and dug a hollow by Surrain's feet. Then they crouched close to the little fairy. Surrain opened her eyes and raised her head. She stared with dismay at the monstrosity that cast a shadow over her wilting body. A cold chill from the angel of death wafted over her, and as the Grim Reaper's black steed reared up Surrain acknowledged defeat. The little fairy gave up and lowered her head.

At that very moment, the contorted branches of the tree holding Surrain unwound. The little fairy fell headlong and cowered beneath the rearing animal. Meanwhile, Becky and Reah were quaking with fear. As the raging beast struck out with his forelegs, the yelping dogs scurried behind a tree.

The rearing horse neighed louder than ever, while the Grim Reaper waved his scythe high above his head and roared, 'Arghhhh! Arghhhhh...!'

Seconds later, horse and rider galloped into the woods, leaving Surrain, Becky and Reah in a state of bewilderment.

On the Brink of Insanity

Bizarre events had unfolded before Surrain's eyes. The little fairy crouched under a tree, beside Becky and Reah. All three, bemused by their recent experience, were alone, but not for long. Becky saw a welcoming sight. She wagged her tail and sighed with relief.

'Ooh at last, Reah, look, Bracken is coming to our rescue.'

A twinkle of hope appeared in Reah's eyes. She smiled, sprang up and quivered with excitement. Bracken landed a few metres away and Reah hurtled towards her. The loving greyhound jumped into Bracken's open arms, causing the plum-haired fairy to fall backwards.

Bracken hugged her dog and cried out, 'Oh, Reah, I love you so much.'

Reah tenderly brushed her head against Bracken and whispered, 'I love you too.'

Bracken sighed. 'I've been searching the woods for ages. Thank goodness you're all safe.'

A streak of jealously ran through Becky's veins and she looked on with envy. Becky suddenly bounded towards Bracken seeking attention.

The plum-haired fairy stroked Becky's curly head. Then Bracken grabbed hold of Becky and uttered, 'Come 'ere you.' Bracken's wings fluttered as she wrapped her arms round Becky and Reah, cuddling them both. 'We're all girls together... my little girlie whirlies. Now let's find out why Surrain has led you a merry dance and brought you out here.'

Reah nuzzled into the plum-haired fairy and said, 'Bracken, it's not Surrain's fault. When she left her party, Orfeo, Veela and Sovran lay snoring. Becky and I couldn't take much more of their heavy breathing, so we decided to join Surrain. And it's a good job we did. Something strange is happening around here and it's affecting Surrain. She isn't herself. Not long ago...'

Then Becky butted in. 'Yeah, Surrain's going loopy, round the twist.'

Reah continued, 'If Surrain doesn't get help soon, she'll go completely mad. The poor girl's been calling me Veela and she thinks Becky is Sovran.'

Becky interrupted Reah again and continued telling the story. 'Surrain has been imagining all sorts of weird things. And a while ago, Reah and I saw ghosts and grinning trees. But w-o-r-s-t of all, we were petrified when the Grim Reaper confronted us. It was... quite awful.'

Bracken shook her head and sighed with disbelief. 'OK. OK. Don't get carried away.' The plum-haired fairy stroked Becky before making her way towards Surrain. Bracken leant over the little fairy and said, 'Surrain, what's wrong?'

Surrain sat on the ground. She gazed at Bracken glassy-eyed and said, 'Whoever you are, please help me... I'm going demented.'

Bracken was taken aback by Surrain's reply and she stood up looking baffled.

Surrain said, 'Princess Debs was here with Prince Daheyl and Prince Deyn. Did you see them?'

'No I didn't and I doubt if you did. Surrain, don't do this to me. Make some sense and stop talking in riddles. You don't even know what Princess Debs and her brothers look like.'

'Of course I do! I've seen their portraits hanging up inside Magentis Castle. Where's the Grim Reaper? Is he coming back for me?' asked Surrain.

Bracken had no idea of Surrain's recent ordeal. She proceeded to lift the little fairy to her feet.

Surrain languished in pain and sighed, 'I can't stand up. The throbbing in my stomach and back is unbearable. Please... Get the wizard.'

Suddenly, the sound of rustling grabbed their attention. Bracken, Becky and Reah turned their heads and peered into the near distance. They caught sight of several shadows moving swiftly round the trees. The atmosphere grew heavy. A horse neighed. Then the group heard a consistent beat striking the ground.

Becky trembled and her voice quivered, 'Ooh, ooh. Bracken, those tiny cloaked beings flying above the Grim Reaper, what are they?'

'Soul collectors,' she replied.

The haunting images and frightening sounds scared them all. Becky and Reah looked round fearfully, their fur standing on end.

For a few moments, Bracken seemed oblivious to the imminent danger. She glared at Becky and said, 'I didn't believe your story earlier, but now I know you were telling me the truth... I'm sorry.'

Becky was overcome with fear and responded abruptly, 'Just get us out of here!'

Reah was of the same mind and yelled, 'Bracken, please don't dither. Time is running out.'

Suddenly, the Grim Reaper's dreaded roar bellowed throughout the woods. As his raging steed charged towards the group, Bracken froze with fear. Then all seemed lost. Surrain, Bracken, Becky and Reah stared in horror at the red-eyed beast racing their way, breathing heavily and snorting flames from his nostrils.

Becky trembled with fear. The poodle braced herself and glared at the oncoming creature. 'Oh no, we're gonna be obliterated. H-e-l-p!' she screamed.

Reah glanced at the plum-haired fairy and yelled, 'Bracken, Bracken, do something Now!'

Reah's plea startled Bracken and she cried out, 'Varishnee sumonere, ambee larr, canis lupus, ambee, ver farr.'

Then, as the black steed leapt over Surrain, Bracken, Becky and Reah, they were engulfed in darkness.

After being in limbo for a time, the two fairies and the dogs found themselves inside Surrain's cottage. Becky and Reah sighed with relief. Both dogs stood upright, hugged each other and danced on the spot singing...

'Hooray hoorah! We're safe we're safe we're safe,
Can't believe we're singing a song, standing face to face...'

Becky and Reah soon realised they were behaving out of character and a serious expression swept across their faces.

The two dogs pushed each other with their paws and Becky shouted, 'Get off me, you dunderhead nincompoop.'

Reah was angry and replied, 'Listen, you poodle-doodle, don't try to humiliate me. The truth is, you're a moronic blockhead, so learn how to behave.'

While Becky and Reah continued to name-call, Bracken helped the little fairy to her feet. Surrain was in agony and barely able to walk.

Bracken sighed and said, 'There's only one place for you, Surrain. Come on let's get you into the bedroom. We'll get your nightwear on and, hopefully, an overnight rest will do you the world of good.'

Once she was in bed Surrain asked Bracken for a drink. 'I'm so thirsty. Could you get me a glass of water please?'

All of a sudden, a jug of water and a glass appeared on the little fairy's bedside table. To Bracken's surprise, Surrain picked up the jug and drank its contents in seconds.

Surrain sighed. 'That's better. I'd be grateful for a refill. I'm incapable of helping myself at the moment.'

'No problem,' said Bracken.

As the jug filled with water, Surrain snuggled under her bed covers. Bracken shook her head in disbelief and made her way out of Surrain's room. The plum-haired fairy promptly joined Becky and Reah, who were still trying to outwit each other.

'Shh,' uttered Bracken. 'Can't you two ever be civil towards each other? Surrain is resting.'

The bickering pair quietened down and Reah glanced at Bracken. 'Is Surrain going to be all right?'

Bracken smiled and replied, 'I hope so.'

Becky sighed. 'We all had mind-blowing experiences in the woods, and Surrain seemed to go crazy.'

'Well, you've got to put those events behind you now. You mustn't get upset and dwell on the past,' said Bracken.

Suddenly, a cluster of stars appeared. As the twinkling lights hovered in the centre of the room, Becky and Reah gulped.

The cream poodle inched her way behind Bracken and whispered, 'When is this creepy stuff going to end?'

Bracken tutted and said, 'What's wrong with you two? Is it stress or what? You should be accustomed to strange phenomena by now. Just watch closely and you'll see what I mean.'

The stars grew bigger. Then, to Becky and Reah's relief, Veela and Sovran materialized. The two wolves seemed taken aback by their arrival and glanced around.

Sovran looked at Veela and said, 'What's going on? We were in limbo, now we're home.'

Veela sighed. 'Sovran, after being confronted by that monstrosity and those creepy ghouls... how can you be so trivial? You know it's magic. Now thank Bracken for bringing us home instead of questioning me.'

The plum-haired fairy was unaware of Veela and Sovran's terrifying encounter with the Grim Reaper and his soul collectors. Due to this and her recent trauma with the dark angel, Veela's remark was overlooked.

'It's OK, Veela,' replied Bracken. Then the plum-haired fairy glanced at Veela and Sovran. 'I uttered a spell and expected you two a while ago. What happened?'

Veela was eager to tell her tale. 'Well, after coming face to face with the Grim Reaper and his hooded cronies, we were shielded by an invisible dome. You know... a so called protection barrier.'

Sovran blurted out, 'We were no match for that entity. One blow from his spiked mace shattered the dome and we were shrouded in darkness.'

Becky and Reah were gobsmacked. 'How did you get out alive?' asked Becky.

'No idea,' replied Veela and Sovran simultaneously.

Reah was concerned about Becky's brother. 'What about Orfeo?' she asked in her soft voice.

Both Veela and Sovran shrugged their shoulders.

Bracken was detached from the situation and unresponsive. Whilst gazing at the two wolves she said, 'Listen, Surrain's had a frightening experience. She's been rambling on about something or other and I can't make any sense of it. Keep an eye on Surrain and I'll pop round early in the morning.'

Veela couldn't understand why Bracken was so distant, but she replied, 'We'll take good care of her.' Veela nudged Sovran, 'Come on slobber chops, we're going to look after Surrain.'

Bracken sighed. 'Now Surrain's in good hands, we must be off. Becky... Reah... are you ready?'

The two dogs were keen to leave and without any hesitation they both replied, 'You bet.'

The trio suddenly vanished. Within seconds they materialized in the woods, beside the fairies, elves, Orfeo and Misty; but Bracken, Becky and Reah were not prepared for the scene that awaited them.

The plum-haired fairy gasped, whilst staring at her companions.

Becky cried out, 'Oh no! What's happened to everyone? Why have they all turned to stone?'

Reah yelled, 'It's the only way they could save themselves. And we thought we had it bad. Bracken, you must release them before that sinister presence reappears.'

While Bracken uttered a spell, Becky and Reah walked cautiously towards their lifeless friends.

Becky whispered, 'Reah, can you feel that crunch underfoot?'

'Yeah, it's the invisible barrier. Sovran did say the Grim Reaper shattered it.'

'Mm he did,' said Becky. Then she shivered, 'Ooh, I don't like this gloomy atmosphere.'

Suddenly, the fairies, elves, Orfeo and Misty stirred. Becky and Reah were delighted. They nuzzled into Orfeo, while the fairies and elves stretched as they rose to their feet.

Nomi smiled and said, 'Thanks for reversing the spell Bracken. Have we got a tale to tell you?'

Laurel shook her head and said, 'Not now, Nomi. Bracken, where's Surrain?'

Bracken sighed deeply. 'She's at home with Veela and Sovran. When I found her she was in a bit of a state. But there's no need to worry. She's in bed and the rest will give her time to recuperate.'

'How bad is Surrain?' asked Jessica.

'Well, she was delirious and asked me to get the wizard. Then dark shadows rushed past the trees and I was distracted. Seconds later the Grim Reaper appeared and his horse charged towards us. The whole experience seems a bit vague, but I suggest we get out of this place pronto.'

'You're right,' replied Laurel. 'I wonder what's wrong with Surrain. She must have forgotten that Wizard J. is out of the kingdom. He's at a Witches Assembly in the Outer Realm of Menoosa.'

Ryar and L.J. stood close together quivering, their faces drained of colour.

Meanwhile, Dayar tried to comfort the youngsters. He became impatient with the fairies and yelled, 'Shut-up. How can you have a conversation when the Grim Reaper and his cronies are out there? Those entities are probably watching us right now. We only stayed in the woods waiting for Surrain, Becky and Reah to return. Now we know what's what, we don't want to stay here a moment longer than we have too, especially after last night. Just look at these two... they're in a state of shock.'

Jessica was more than curious and she cried out, 'Why? What happened?'

'Never mind about that now,' replied Dayar. 'Hopefully we'll live to tell the tale another day.'

Nomi was taken aback, 'Dayar, don't get so irate. Everything will be back to normal tomorrow... I promise. Right, my priority is to get you three back home... so here goes.' Nomi proceeded with the spell. The elves vanished and appeared safely in their homes. Then Nomi looked at her friends. 'I suggest we meet in Surrain's cottage shortly after dawn and have a yatter about today's experience.'

The fairies agreed. Seconds later Laurel, Nomi, Bracken and Jessica wished each other farewell and, within an instant, the fairies and their animals also vanished.

Darkness descended and during the dead of night, unearthly souls roamed the fairy kingdom. Doleful wolf-cries echoed throughout the land, while phantoms searched for their next victim...

An Eerie Presence

It was the crack of dawn. As the morning sun began to rise, the cockerel's cry woke Reah. The greyhound lifted her head and caught sight of Bracken snoring. Reah curled up and continued to sleep. Time passed quickly and the clock struck 7am. Reah jumped up, her eyes bloodshot with lack of sleep. She felt edgy. Something was wrong.

The anxious greyhound nudged Bracken and cried out, 'Wake-up. We should be at Surrain's.'

Bracken, bleary-eyed and tired, replied, 'Ooh, is it morning already?'

'Yes. And we've overslept... It's past 7am.'

The plum-haired fairy snuggled into her duvet and sighed. 'I've had an awful sleep. I've been dreaming about ghosts, ghouls, howling wolves and cries from children of the night.'

'That was no dream,' replied Reah. Then she gripped the duvet with her teeth and pulled it off the bed. 'Come on Bracken. You told Veela and Sovran you'd be round early to check on Surrain.'

'So I did Reah... Give me a moment to freshen up.'

Seconds later Bracken was ready to leave and she uttered a spell. Bracken and Reah appeared near Surrain's cottage, which was shrouded in light mist. As the pair made their way along the little fairy's path, Reah stopped dead in her tracks.

Bracken glanced at Reah, her heart pounding. 'Reah, what are you staring at?'

The greyhound whispered, 'Look at the window on the right. That tall dark figure isn't Surrain.'

Bracken was anxious and replied, 'I can't see anything. Ooh, you've got me all jittery now.' The plum-haired fairy knocked on Surrain's door... there was nothing but an eerie silence. 'That's strange. Come on, Reah, we're going in.'

The front door was unlocked so Bracken walked cautiously towards Surrain's living room with Reah close at her heels. Bracken peered round the half-open door into the cold room.

Reah gulped and whispered, 'Ooh it's so gloomy in here. I've got a bad feeling about this.'

Bracken shivered. She reached her hand down and stroked Reah's head. 'I know. It feels quite spooky.'

Surrain's cottage was all on one level. Bracken stepped across the hallway towards the little fairy's bedroom.

Suddenly, a tall figure wearing a black hooded cloak appeared beside Bracken.

Reah could sense the eerie presence and as her fur stood on end, she shuddered. Reah whispered, 'Bracken, this is too creepy for me. I'm out of here.' Then Reah turned and scrambled across the wooden floor, towards the open door.

Bracken was scared, nevertheless she continued. At that time, the plum-haired fairy was unaware of an evil entity gliding alongside her. Bracken rubbed her ice-cold hands together and crept into Surrain's bedroom.

Reah, as anxious as ever, paced the garden waiting for Bracken.

All of a sudden, Bracken dashed out of the cottage with tears streaming down her cheeks. The plum-haired fairy sat on the step dabbing her watery eyes. Reah was about to ask Bracken what was wrong, but she didn't have a chance. Laurel, Nomi and Jessica had arrived on the scene.

Meanwhile, Becky and Orfeo joined Reah. The animals sat together whispering while the fairies questioned Bracken.

'What's the matter?' asked Laurel.

Bracken wiped away her tears and replied, 'I looked at Surrain and... She's... She's...'

'She's what?' cried Laurel.

Nomi and Jessica rushed into the cottage. When they entered Surrain's bedroom, Veela and Sovran lay quietly by the bed. The wolves barely moved, but their eyes followed the two fairies round the room.

Surrain's quilt reached her neck and she looked as if she was sleeping peacefully.

Then Nomi and Jessica took a closer look. They glanced at each other and said, 'Surrain's got spots.'

Nomi and Jessica felt uncomfortable inside Surrain's room. The nervous pair didn't want to wait around and they hurried out of the cottage.

Laurel was apprehensive, expecting the worst. 'Well?' she asked, waiting for an answer.

'Surrain's got a few green spots,' replied Jessica.

Laurel tutted. 'Bracken, what is the matter with you?'

Once again tears rolled down Bracken's cheeks. The plum-haired fairy raised her head and stared at Laurel, Nomi and Jessica. 'It's not me. It's you lot. Can't you see there's something wrong? And don't you think it's strange that Veela and Sovran are in low spirits? Just before I entered Surrain's bedroom, there was a horrible atmosphere, and a cold chill hit me. That feeling brought to mind a chain of events that happened to me many years ago, and I'm still affected by them.'

Laurel sighed. 'Mm I remember. But Bracken, this is different.'

A look of despair filled Bracken's eyes and she cried out, 'No it's not different. Earlier I cast a spell in Surrain's bedroom. I tried to remove the evil presence... instead the atmosphere grew really heavy. It freaked me out and left the place as fast as I could.'

Nomi was listening intently, staring at Bracken. Then she shouted, 'I was aware of two ghoulish fiends.'

Jessica blurted out, 'So was I. The bad spirits clouded Surrain's bedroom and drove us out.'

Unbeknown to the fairies, Becky, Orfeo and Reah were standing beside them listening to the conversation. The three dogs knew Surrain was alive. Nevertheless, they sensed fear and looked tense.

Bracken fumbled about with her handkerchief, occasionally dabbing her nose. The plum-haired fairy leant to her left and glanced behind her friends. Nomi and Jessica were extremely jumpy. They spun round, and sighed with relief when they saw the elf messengers approaching.

Nomi whispered, 'Shh... Surrain is sleeping. I'll take her post.'

Dayar frowned and said, 'Surrain hasn't got any messages today, nor has anyone else. We've called to see if Surrain is any better and to wish her well.'

Jessica smiled. 'Aw, that's really thoughtful of you. The thing is, Surrain is still off colour and we've left her sleeping.'

'Is there anything we can do to help?' asked Dayar.

'No,' replied Laurel. 'It's nice of you to offer, but everything's in hand.'

L.J. had an inquiring mind and he looked straight at Jessica. 'Why is Bwacken snivelling?' he asked.

Jessica was quick to reply. She grabbed hold of L.J. and whispered in his ear. 'It's a girlie thing.'

Nomi said, 'Why don't you call round tomorrow? It doesn't matter if Surrain has no messages. I'm sure she'll be much better by then. And she'll be pleased to see you.'

Dayar nodded and replied, 'OK.'

A look of disappointment filled the elves' faces and they walked back down the path.

Ryar whispered, 'The fairies want us out of the way. They're definitely hiding something.'

'Mm,' uttered L.J. 'Suwwain must be weally ill... or... what if she's dead?'

Dayar cried out, 'L.J. shut-up. You can't speculate on these matters!'

The young elf's lip quivered and he began to cry. In a trembling voice he said, 'I just want to see Suwwain.'

Dayar comforted L.J. and replied, 'I'm sorry L.J. I didn't mean to shout. Don't upset yourself. We'll go round to Surrain's tomorrow morning.'

Back at the cottage Nomi chuckled. She nudged Jessica and said, 'Fancy you telling the elves that Surrain's off colour.'

'Well she is ill. And you've got to admit, Surrain's complexion does have a green tinge.'

Laurel tutted and sighed. 'I've heard enough. I'm going to see Surrain for myself. Are you three coming along or what?' she asked abruptly.

Nomi, Bracken and Jessica followed Laurel. They crept into Surrain's bedroom and the cold hit them. As the fairies shuddered, small clouds of mist frosted the air.

Nomi's eyes widened and she scanned the room. 'Can you feel that heaviness?' she asked.

Jessica glanced towards the window and quietly replied, 'Yeah. There's something horrible in here.'

As Laurel shivered, she said, 'This cold will be the death of Surrain. We've got to get her into the living room.'

Just then, Surrain opened her eyes. 'Why are you three creeping round and whispering?'

The fairies gasped and Jessica said, 'We didn't want to wake you.'

When Laurel saw Surrain's face dotted with green spots, she was alarmed by her condition and she asked herself, "Is this blight? Ooh how can this be? But Surrain isn't showing the obvious symptoms." Laurel wanted to be sure, so for the time being, she didn't share her thoughts.

Surrain struggled to sit up, so Bracken gave her a helping hand. 'Let me plump up your pillows,' she said. Then Bracken sat on the edge of the bed. 'You don't look yourself at all. How do you feel?'

Surrain smiled, 'I'm OK. Just a little tired with the self-inflicted aches and pains from dancing. One thing puzzles me though.'

Nomi sat beside Surrain and took hold of her hand. 'And what's that?'

Surrain frowned and replied, 'Well, I remember dancing... and after that my memory is a blur.'

Bracken sighed. 'Surrain, yesterday you wandered off without telling a soul. I found you deep in the woods with Becky and Reah by your side. You were doubled up in pain and asked me to get Wizard Jozeffri.'

Surrain was surprised. 'I don't remember. Ooh, I must have been out of it, because I know J. was at a Witches Assembly in Menoosa.' Surrain held her head in her hands. 'Ooh,' she gasped. 'I've just had a flash back... I remember seeing black shadows darting amongst the trees. And faces... faces coming at me! What happened out there?'

Bracken shook her head and sighed, 'We don't know.'

After a moment, Surrain looked towards her bedside table, into the empty jug. 'I'm so hot and thirsty. Could I have a cool drink and a flannel rinsed out in cold water?'

Jessica stood up. 'Sure. I'll get you the facecloth.'

As Jessica left the room, Bracken uttered a spell and the jug filled to the brim with cold water. Surrain took hold of the container with both hands and drank its contents in one go. Bracken wasn't surprised, but Nomi and Laurel looked on in disbelief.

Nomi cried out, 'Surrain, I've never seen you do such a thing.'

'Well I've never craved water before. I told you, I'm really hot and I feel parched.'

Bracken sighed. 'Never mind about that... Listen Surrain, you won't get any better sleeping in this room, it's absolutely freezing.' The plum-haired fairy rose to her feet and walked towards the window. Then she scraped her nails down the frosty coating and said, 'Look, the glass is covered with ice.'

Laurel cringed and screeched, 'Ooh Bracken, don't do that. The noise is going through me.'

Bracken didn't care. She found her actions amusing, and chuckled to herself as she continued to scratch the frosted glass. All of sudden Bracken was overcome with fear, and her expression changed. She shivered and rushed towards the bed uttering, 'Ooh my blood has just ran cold.' Bracken was clearly distressed and perched on the edge of the bed looking straight at the little fairy. 'Surrain, you're hot because you have a fever. Now will you go in the living room and rest on the sofa?'

Surrain, as stubborn as ever, quietly replied, 'No. I'm comfy where I am.'

The two wolves, who hadn't budged all morning, peered up at the fairies, looking dejected.

Jessica returned with the flannel. As she approached Surrain's bedroom, the blonde haired fairy froze on the spot. Surrain's bed was to the left behind the open door, so the fairies couldn't see Jessica. The tomboy fairy's sensitivity enabled her to see a terrifying incarnation, the Crimson Cut-throat, standing by the window opposite the doorway. The evil entity waved his cut-throat razor at Jessica, while a number of soul collectors flitted about his head. The Crimson Cut-throat glided swiftly towards her and straight through her body. Jessica stood rigid and trembled as she closed her eyes. When she opened them again, all the spirits were gone. Realising that her friends hadn't seen the phantoms, she put on a brave face and walked into the room.

'About time,' cried Bracken.

Jessica ignored Bracken and gave Surrain the flannel, 'There we are,' she said cheerfully.

As Surrain mopped her brow, Laurel glanced at Jessica and said, 'What's up Jess? You're as white as a ghost.'

Jessica tried to repress her fear, and as she quivered her teeth chattered. 'I'm f-fine. It's j-just so c-cold in here. Surrain, while you're ill we'll stay with you. And if you're no b-better tomorrow, we'll get the s-sorceress. Come on, let's g-get you in the other room. I've built up a fire, so it's quite cosy in there.'

At last Surrain had come to her senses. 'All right,' she said. 'I want you all to know, I do appreciate everything you're doing for me.'

Surrain wrapped the duvet around herself and, with the help of her friends she was soon comfortable on the sofa. Veela and Sovran followed and lay on the rug with sadness in their eyes, staring into the roaring fire.

Seconds later, Nomi perched on the edge of the sofa by Surrain's feet. 'Do you want anything?'

'Yes please. Could you get Wonda? She's on the windowsill in the kitchen.'

'Of course...' Nomi returned in no time and gave Surrain the tiny wand.

'Thanks, Nomi. Wonda is invaluable while I'm under the weather and powerless.'

Nomi sighed. 'I know Surrain, but we are here to help you too.'

The little fairy smiled, closed her eyes and snuggled under her cover.

'I'm nipping home to feed Misty,' whispered Laurel. 'I'll be back before you know it.'

Just then, Veela spoke quietly to Sovran and both wolves rose to their feet.

Sovran glanced at Laurel and said, 'Can we join Becky, Orfeo and Reah outside?'

'Sure,' replied Laurel. 'And when I return, I'll feed you lot under the veranda.'

Laurel made her way outside followed by Veela and Sovran. A moment later, Laurel vanished.

'What shall we do to while away the time?' asked Nomi.

Bracken thought for a second and said, 'What about playing Tekwah's Star, chess or cards?'

Jessica quickly replied, 'Good idea. We'll play Tekwah's Star.' Suddenly, the game appeared in Jessica's hands.

Bracken giggled. 'You and that game Jessica. I'm sure you're addicted to it.'

After a short time, Laurel materialized. 'All done... The animals are fed, so we just have Surrain and ourselves to look after.' Then Laurel frowned. 'Jess, what are you doing playing Tekwah's Star?'

'It was my suggestion,' cried Bracken. 'We can't twiddle our thumbs and yatter until dawn. So I thought we'd keep an eye on Surrain, sit by the fire and play games.'

Laurel sighed. 'Fine, as long as we're quiet. Surrain is sleeping peacefully, so let's keep it that way.'

The fairies began to feel at home and a pleasant ambience filled the room.

Nomi uttered a spell. All of a sudden an oversized bed, complete with a duvet and pillows, appeared behind the sofa. Nomi smiled and jumped on the bed. 'This is what I call comfort.'

There was a ripple of giggles as the fairies settled down to entertain themselves....

Darkness descended on the kingdom and the fairies drifted to sleep... Once again during the dead of night, howling wolf cries echoed throughout the land.

Dawn was breaking and Bracken was the first to stir. She fluttered her wings and flew off the bed, trying not to disturb her friends. The plum-haired fairy landed near the fireside chair. She had a peek at Surrain and smiled to herself. "All seems well." Then Bracken kicked over an empty jug and said, 'I don't remember that being there. And what's this?' Bracken picked up Surrain's book of poems and began to flick through the pages. She was intrigued and sat in the little fairy's fireside chair reading Surrain's heartfelt verses.

Nomi yawned and sat up. 'What are you reading Bracken?' she asked.

The plum-haired fairy was eager to show Nomi and flew onto the bed. 'Surrain's written a number of poems and the title is quite fitting, Emotions of the Heart.' Then Bracken sighed. 'It's these last verses that are puzzling me. Here, read them and tell me what you think.'

Nomi ran her eyes over the poem and said, 'Mm... Have you taken a look at Surrain today?'

'Yeah, I had a peek at her earlier and there seems to be an improvement.'

Nomi smiled. 'That's good... It's just, this poem is mystifying. By the way, what time is it?'

'Gone 8.30,' replied Bracken.

Nomi sighed, 'Already? I'll wake Laurel in a minute and point out Surrain's last poem. Then she can give me her opinion.'

'OK. I'm just going outside to see Reah and the other animals.'

The three dogs and two wolves stood up when Bracken approached. They were uneasy and eager to know if the little fairy's condition had grown any worse.

Reah was aware of Bracken's inner turmoil and she nuzzled into the fairy. 'How is Surrain?'

Then Veela looked up at Bracken with sorrow in her eyes. 'Yes, is Surrain any better? After the recent events, we're extremely worried.'

Bracken knelt down. She stroked all the animals and said, 'Well, yesterday Surrain had a fever and green spots covering her face. But today her complexion is blemish-free. So I'm sure she'll be fine.'

Sovran sighed. 'Oh that's a relief. But now we're confused,' he said. 'We haven't been able to relax, because we sense a dark force hovering around Surrain.'

Bracken nodded her head. 'I know. There is a sinister presence lurking about.'

'Be wary, Bracken, and please take care of Surrain,' said Orfeo.

'Don't worry, boy. I will.'

Then Becky added, 'News about Surrain's illness is sweeping the forest. What can we do to stop the word spreading?'

'You can't do anything,' replied Bracken. 'As soon as Surrain recovers, her appearance will put an end to that. Right, little ones, I'm going back inside the cottage and I'll see you later.'

By now Laurel and Jessica had woken up. They were still in bed and reading through Surrain's verses.

Jessica sighed. 'I'm baffled. Why should Surrain write a poem called Letting Go?'

Nomi shook her head and replied, 'I don't know. Maybe it was due to the sickness that attacked Surrain... she was hallucinating.'

'Mm... Seems plausible,' said Bracken. 'Becky and Reah did say Surrain had been suffering from illusions.'

'Well there you are!' exclaimed Nomi. 'And she's been exhausted lately.'

Bracken sat in Surrain's fireside chair and watched the little fairy as she slept on. 'Surrain looks so peaceful.'

Laurel had been thinking deeply. She closed Surrain's little book and said, 'I can't put my finger on it, but there's more to this last poem than meets the eye.'

'What should we do?' asked Bracken.

Nomi sighed. 'If Surrain isn't quite herself in an hour or so, we'd better seek Vienne's help.'

Bracken stood up, took the book from Laurel and placed it on a small table. 'I hope it doesn't come to that.'

'Let's be optimistic and look on the bright side,' cried Jessica. 'If Surrain was at death's door, the sorceress would have been here yesterday.'

Laurel nodded. 'I agree with you, Jess. But saying that, there is something really weird going on.'

The Mystery Deepens

Nomi, Laurel, Bracken and Jessica kept a watchful eye on Surrain. Meanwhile, the residents at Magentis Castle were unaware of Surrain's worsening condition.

Sian and Fee were as happy as could be, fulfilling their castle duties in an effortless way. The giggling pair fluttered in and out of certain rooms, sprucing up the fortress with the flick of a finger.

The time was approaching 9am when the three elf messengers arrived at Magentis Castle.

Dayar, Ryar and L.J. walked through the entrance hall towards the stairs. Suddenly, loud clumpy footsteps were heard and the elves glanced to their right. Greega straightened his eye patch and walked towards the youngsters, but the elves barely took any notice of the guard.

Greega wanted to alert the elves, so he shouted in his gruff voice, alarming them, 'Elves... Be still!'

Dayar, Ryar and L.J. were startled by Greega's aggressiveness, especially as they'd been good. The elves froze on the spot and stared up at the guard.

Greega said, 'Prince Tal wants to see you immediately. Follow me and don't dawdle.' Greega started up the stairs and when he reached the ninth step he turned round and yelled, 'Make haste! This is an urgent matter.'

The three elves didn't question the Dog Man. Even though Greega could be pleasant and helpful, he was respected but positively feared. As the elves hurried along, they glanced at each other with worried expressions, wondering what they'd done wrong.

Greega knocked on Prince Tal's door, while Dayar, Ryar and L.J. stood quaking behind him.

'Enter,' said the Prince. The Dog Man promptly opened the door. 'Thank you, Greega. Show the elves in.'

The youngsters shuffled into the room while Greega closed the door and waited outside.

Prince Tal sat at his desk and continued to write for a few seconds. 'I won't keep you,' he mumbled. A moment later, the Prince placed his quill in the stand and looked across at the elves. 'There's no need to huddle together and look so nervous... you haven't committed treason. Right,' he sighed. 'I'll come straight to the point. Did Surrain receive my letter? If so... did Surrain give you a reply?'

There was silence. Besides being puzzled by the two questions, the elves felt an instant sense of relief.

'Well?!' exclaimed the Prince. 'I'm waiting for an answer to simple questions.'

The three youngsters gulped and Dayar replied, 'Erm, yes, Sir.'

Prince Tal cried out, 'Yes Sir what? Come on, Dayar, spit it out.'

'Yes, Sir, Surrain received your letter and gave me an instant reply.'

'So where is the letter? And why didn't you bring it to me that very evening?'

The elves were stumped by this question and bit their lips.

Dayar tried to explain. 'Sir, due to unexpected circumstances, we had to make a detour round the woods. When we finally reached the castle it was dark and we couldn't find you. The only other option was to put the envelope on the message table.'

Before anyone had time to think, Ryar blurted out, 'The hooded skeleton terrified us. And when that evil entity tried to kill us, Dayar confronted him.'

Then L.J. joined in. 'Sir, the Grim Reaper came after us on his massive black horse. So we ran like mad through the woods.'

Ryar added, 'Yeah... that gruesome being was relentless and we couldn't escape.'

L.J. continued, 'Sir, the Grim Reaper zapped Dayar and blue flashes flickered along Dayar's body electrocuting me and Ryar. We were nearly goners, Sir, nearly deaduns!'

Prince Tal's thoughts were elsewhere and he sighed, 'Mm... I suppose that accounts for your blue hair?' The Prince leaned forward across his desk and asked L.J. a question. 'Tell me, L.J. Who did you say was chasing you?'

L.J. raised his eyebrows. He moved his face closer to the Prince and whispered, 'Sir, it was the Grim Reaper, riding his scary black horse.'

Prince Tal smiled. 'Well, well. I see the elixir from Sorceress Vienne has worked a treat.'

L.J. was stuck for words, but Dayar chuckled and ruffled the youngster's bright blue hair. 'Hey, L.J., that's great.'

Ryar nudged his cousin. 'Ooh... And we didn't even notice. Hey L.J., repeat this rhyme after me... There was a red robin called Oscar, who had a feathery friend called Roster. The owl and red robin r...'

Prince Tal banged his hand on the desk top. 'That's enough, Ryar. And I've heard enough about the Grim Reaper. If that entity was seeking elves, you wouldn't be here to tell the tale.' Then Prince Tal beckoned the elves and whispered, 'The angel of death sits on his horse, watching and waiting... festering in the shadows. When he's ready... he POUNCES on his next victim!'

The youngsters jumped back and gasped, while the Prince burst out laughing, 'That got you going.'

Prince Tal's tone changed. 'Now, let's get back to Surrain's reply. I still haven't received the letter. What's more...I've been waiting patiently for the last few days. So, Dayar, you said you left the letter on the message table? Come on, we'll take a look and you can retrace your movements.'

As Prince Tal walked towards the door, Ryar pulled at Dayar's arm and whispered, 'I saw you place the envelope underneath the paperweight.'

Dayar shushed his brother. Then the elves and Greega followed Prince Tal down the hallway. They stopped by the small round-top table.

The Prince stood with folded arms and said, 'Right, Dayar, show me exactly where you left Surrain's letter.'

Dayar took hold of the paperweight and placed his other hand in the centre of the table. 'I definitely put the envelope here and slid the paperweight over the top to secure it.'

Prince Tal shook his head. 'I remember that night well. We had gale-force winds. But that's nothing to do with the letter vanishing. Oh, I don't know...' He sighed. 'This is turning out to be a complete mystery. Right, boys, search the area and there's not a corner to be missed.'

Dayar and Ryar moved the message table. They searched on their hands and knees while Prince Tal, L.J. and Greega walked towards the long red drapes.

Prince Tal glanced at the guard and said, 'Greega, let's have some more light up here.'

Greega drew back the curtains and beams of sunlight shone through the stained glass window.

Dayar and Ryar were still looking high and low for the letter...however, nothing was found. The pair abandoned the search and sat at the top of the stairs wondering what to do next.

Meanwhile, L.J. rummaged behind the drapes, twisting them around himself as he ran his fingers along the hem.

Moments later, everyone heard bumps and bangs coming from Meidi's room. The Grand Master opened his door and heads turned to the right of the landing. Meidi glared at Dayar and Ryar with a furious expression. 'What's all the damn noise? And why are you blue-haired morons sitting on the stairs doing nothing?' he yelled.

The two elves were at a loss for words. They jumped to their feet and stared at Meidi with blank expressions.

The Grand Master was seething with anger and continued to shout. 'And you boy...! Stop swinging on the curtains. What's going on? Is there no control around here...?'

Little L.J. peered at Meidi from behind the twirling curtains. As the pale-faced elf tried to keep still, the curtains speedily unwound. And L.J. cried out, 'Arghhhh.' Seconds later he was in a heap on the floor.

Greega was some way from L.J. He stood upright and silent. The guard took Meidi's explosion of anger in his stride and, in this instance, he knew better than to utter a word.

Prince Tal on the other hand was annoyed and quickly responded. 'Meidi, we're not making any noise whatsoever. All we're doing is searching the area for a letter that's gone astray. A letter addressed to me.'

The Grand Master reached into his pocket and said, 'Is this what you're looking for?'

Prince Tal walked up to Meidi and took the envelope, 'Yes, this is the one,' he replied. 'What possessed you to hold onto my letter for three days?'

Meidi lowered his head and in a feeble manner he said, 'You know I've been absent-minded lately... I forgot, simple as that.' Then he snarled, 'I'm not to blame. It was one of those little cretins who shoved the envelope under my door.'

By this time Prince Tal was extremely angry. He glared at Meidi and defended the elves, giving the Grand Master a taste of his own medicine. 'Meidi, you're ruler of this kingdom, but at times you are despicable. Don't you ever criticize or speak badly of these three youngsters again. They are the most hard-working, helpful and trustworthy elves in the kingdom. And I assure you...they did Not push My letter under Your door.'

Meidi scowled and his top lip quivered. Then he stomped into his room and slammed the door.

Greega watched and listened to everything. The guard stood straight-faced and motionless, although he wanted to jump for joy when Prince Tal put Meidi in his place.

Dayar, Ryar and L.J. were unnerved by the incident and rushed towards the Prince.

L.J. couldn't hold back his feelings and cried out, 'Meidi scared the living daylights out of us.'

Prince Tal wrapped his arms around the elves' shoulders and consoled them. 'Meidi shouldn't frighten or belittle you three. Huh, he's such a cantankerous so and so at times.'

'Thanks for defending us, Sir,' said Dayar.

Ryar added, 'Yes Sir, thanks for being on our side.'

Prince Tal smiled and replied, 'I wouldn't have it any other way.'

'At least you've got your message, Sir,' said L.J.

'Mm,' said the Prince. 'Still... I'm baffled. One mystery unfolds, and another is created. Mark my words, the mystery surrounding the resting place of this letter will come to light soon and the riddle will be solved. Now, boys, let me get on and read Surrain's reply.'

Within seconds the Prince folded the note and put it in his pocket.

'Sir... is everything to your satisfaction?' asked Greega.

Prince Tal tapped the guard on his shoulder and replied, 'Yes thanks, Greega. Right, I'm off to see Vienne to get my amulet filled up. Then I'm going straight to Surrain's... we have a lot of catching up to do. Greega my man... I'm using magic dust to get to my destination and I don't know what time I'll be returning. So could you look in on Jameela and make sure she's OK?'

'Certainly Sir...'

Prince Tal hurried off, leaving Dayar, Ryar and L.J. standing on the upper landing beside Greega.

All of a sudden Ryar grabbed Dayar's arm, 'Oh no!' he exclaimed. 'We forgot to tell the Prince about Surrain's illness.'

Greega leant over the elves and his deep voice bellowed down their ears, 'What's this I hear about the little fairy?'

Dayar replied, 'Greega, Surrain's really ill.' Then the youngster began to explain. 'Two days ago during fairy festivity, Surrain wandered into the woods with Becky and Reah. When the fairies realised Surrain and the two dogs were missing, Bracken went to search for them. Bracken found Surrain disorientated, in a state of delirium. Now the fairies are looking after her. We're going to Surrain's later, to see if she's any better. We just came here to check the message table, to see if there was any post to deliver on the way.'

Greega looked somewhat perplexed. 'Dayar, how do you know Surrain was delirious?'

'Well, we were with the fairies when Bracken returned...without Surrain. Apparently, Surrain was totally confused and rambling on, so Bracken took her straight home.'

'This is really important,' said Greega. 'Do you know what the fairies were eating?'

'Mushrooms,' replied Dayar. 'They were eating the mound of mushrooms they'd collected. You know... it's their party thing isn't it?'

A worried look swept across Greega's wrinkled face. 'Yes it is,' he sighed. 'I'm sorry to ask you all these questions, only it's vital I have the correct information. Have you any idea when Surrain began to behave in this strange way?'

The three elves didn't say a word. They shrugged their shoulders and glanced at each other.

Then Greega continued. 'I'll put it another way. Do any of you remember the events that took place before Surrain wandered off? And had the fairies finished eating?'

Ryar raised his hand and shouted out, 'Yes they'd all eaten. I remember that 'cause we were watching from the treetop. We heard

Taz telling stories and when she finished, all the fairies danced. Then Taz and Shadow left for Drakohsia. Soon after, Surrain wandered into the woods.'

Dayar added, 'We joined the fairies a bit later, but we didn't eat. There was nothing left.'

L.J. said, 'Dayar and Ryar forgot to tell you about the Grim Reaper and the Soul Collectors. When Bracken went to search for Surrain, those evil spirits came after us. They tried to kill us three, the fairies and their animals, so Nomi turned us all to stone. Does that help?'

Greega stroked his chin and looked rather solemn. 'As a matter of fact it does help. Thank you,' he replied. 'Now I need you to think back and answer one more question. Did any of you hear the little fairy cough?'

The elves shook their heads. Not one of them could recall Surrain coughing.

The silence was suddenly broken by Sian and Fee. The singing duo flew up the stairs, fluttering above Greega and the elves. Sian was surprised to see such miserable faces, but Feebee was annoyed. She thought the youngsters were avoiding their duties.

Sian smiled, 'Good morning. And what's with the gloomy atmosphere on such a beautiful day?'

Greega was about to answer Sian, when Feebee jumped into the conversation.

Fee rubbed her hands together and said, 'We're all done and dusted.' Then she glanced at Greega and the elves. 'Huh, look at you four. You look as glum as could be. I've seen happier faces at a funeral. And you elves should be getting a move on, instead of wasting the morning yattering.'

'Get lost,' cried Ryar. 'You're not our boss, so don't be telling us what to do.'

Feebee was taken aback by Ryar's outburst and gasped. 'Well I never.'

L.J. scowled at Fee, while Dayar placed his arm across Ryar's shoulder and whispered, 'Calm down, Ryar. Just ignore her.' Dayar glanced at the two fairies and said, 'I take it you're not aware of Surrain's illness?'

Sian and Feebee looked at Dayar with serious expressions.

'What illness? When did this happen?' asked Sian.

Dayar shrugged his shoulders and sighed, 'It's a mystery.'

Then Greega stepped in. 'When I asked the elves a particular question, they didn't know the answer. Maybe one of you could help.'

'Fire away,' said Fee.

'Did either of you hear Surrain cough during your festivity?'

'I did,' replied Sian. 'Surrain definitely coughed. In fact she began to choke and Nomi banged her on the back. You recall that, don't you, Fee? Don't you, Feebee?'

'Yes... Yes sorry I was thinking. You're right, Sian.'

'Thanks for your help,' said Greega. As the guard rushed down the stairs, he cried out, 'This illness sounds gravely familiar. So I must see Surrain for myself. I just hope I'm wrong.'

Greega knew Prince Tal hadn't taken Jameela, so the Dog Man headed for the stables.

Meanwhile, Fee stood with her hands on her hips. 'Well, that was nice I don't think. If Greega had waited for a moment, he could have been at Surrain's in an instant. Huh, seems like he prefers the mortal way.' Feebee turned to the elves and said, 'Right, boys, Sian and I are off to see Surrain. Do you want to come with us?'

Ryar and L.J. smiled, while Dayar replied, 'Yes, please.'

Fee didn't waste any time. She uttered a spell and the two fairies along with the three elves vanished.

An Explosion of Anger

Within seconds of vanishing from Magentis Castle, Sian, Fee, Dayar, Ryar and L.J. appeared in Surrain's garden. The fairies and elves made their way towards Becky, Orfeo and Reah who were sitting together.

Sian leaned over to Feebee and whispered, 'I don't like this eerie atmosphere. There's definitely something creepy around.'

Feebee was curious and asked Orfeo a question, 'Do you know if Surrain is all right?'

The black poodle glanced at Fee and replied, 'As far as we know. Bracken came out of the cottage earlier and told us that Surrain had improved.'

A look of surprise swept across Sian's face and she cried out, 'Ooh that's a relief. I'm glad Surrain's on the mend. It's just...we saw Greega a little while ago and he seemed really worried about her.'

'Come on, Sian, let's go inside and say hello,' said Feebee.

Reah took a deep breath and softly whispered, 'I don't think that's a good idea.'

Feebee turned her head. She was uppish and replied abruptly, 'Why not?'

Reah didn't say a word. The greyhound lowered her head and shied away.

Feebee's hoity-toity manner annoyed Becky who was quick to respond. The poodle walked in front of the fairy, stuck her muzzle in the air, and mimicked Feebee in an ear-piercing tone, 'Why is not a zed...you haughty redhead!'

Fee scowled and pointed at Becky yelling, 'You acrimonious cream frizzle. Watch your tongue or you'll be a sizzle!' Feebee promptly linked Sian and tugged at her arm, 'Come along.'

As the two fairies approached the cottage door, they heard Prince Tal talking.

Feebee turned round and stared at Becky. 'You didn't tell me the Prince was in there.'

Becky smirked and said, 'Well you didn't ask me, did you?'

Veela and Sovran, who were standing outside the front door, glanced at each other.

Then Sian spoke directly to Veela. 'When did Prince Tal arrive?'

'The Prince turned up a few seconds before you. And he stormed into the cottage.'

Sian and Feebee walked under the veranda. Moments later, the two fairies were joined by Dayar, Ryar and L.J. They all took a peek through the side window, where they heard Prince Tal shouting at the fairies.

'Not one of you had the decency to let me know Surrain was ill. And seriously ill at that! What's wrong with you lot?' Nomi, Laurel, Bracken and Jessica stood in silence, while the Prince continued to bellow. 'Open the windows and let some air in here... No wonder Surrain is not responding, you're suffocating her.'

Sian, Fee and the three elves looked closely through the glass, trying to catch a glimpse of Surrain. Then they saw Laurel walking towards them. Without any hesitation, they ducked down out of sight.

Laurel didn't see a soul and, uttering groans of disapproval, she opened the window.

'What are you muttering, Laurel?' cried the Prince.

Laurel replied with a sigh, 'Surrain has a fever, so we kept all the windows closed... That's all.'

Bracken blurted out, 'We were waiting to see how Surrain was feeling. And if she wasn't quite herself, we were going to fetch Vienne.'

Prince Tal sighed. 'Well at this moment in time, the sorceress is unable to help anyone.'

'Why?' asked Jessica.

'I'll tell you later,' replied the Prince.

Nomi picked up Surrain's wand. The fairy made her way to the kitchen and before she placed Wonda on the windowsill, she whispered, 'Wonda... is there any way you can help Surrain?'

Suddenly, a tiny head popped out of the black rod and Wonda looked at Nomi. 'Sadly I cannot help. There are powerful forces upon us... entities from above and beyond. All we can do is hope.'

Tears rolled down Nomi's cheeks. She wiped her eyes and returned to the living room.

Prince Tal leaned over the little fairy. He was about to lift Surrain off the sofa when Bracken cried out, 'What do you think you're doing?'

'I beg your pardon? What does it look like?' yelled the Prince. 'I'm taking Surrain into the other room where she'll be more comfortable. Now open the bedroom door.'

The fairies were determined to keep Surrain out of her bedroom, so Laurel stepped in front of the closed door. 'Surrain's not going in there. That room is bitterly cold due to an evil presence.'

'That's nonsense,' shouted the Prince. He pushed Laurel out of the way and opened the door himself. 'What cold?' asked Prince Tal as he walked into the bedroom, 'It's actually warm in here...I'm going to get Surrain.'

Just then Bracken entered the bedroom. The plum-haired fairy turned full circle and laughed aloud. 'It's true,' she cried. 'The sun is beaming through the windows and there's no evidence of ghostly activity whatsoever.'

Prince Tal lifted Surrain off the sofa and carried her frail body into the bedroom. As the Prince wrapped the quilt around Surrain, she opened her eyes and smiled. Prince Tal sat on the edge of the bed and held Surrain's hand. Meanwhile, Nomi, Laurel, Bracken and Jessica stood near the door.

To the surprise of the four fairies, Prince Tal began to tell them about his recent conversation with the sorceress. 'I called upon Vienne earlier. She was greatly troubled, which is most unlike her...and I couldn't understand why. After a few moments, the sorceress opened up and described her vision... Just before I arrived at Vienne's home, she was scrying and the clear water suddenly darkened. The sorceress saw Surrain lying motionless in bed, and she was not alone. The angel sitting on Surrain's right shoulder was surrounded by white light, but the angel sitting on Surrain's left shoulder, was shrouded in darkness. In this instance, these images signify the fight for survival... even death. And it doesn't end there. As Vienne filled my sacred amulet with magic dust, she told me powerful entities were present in the kingdom, and these formidable forces rendered her powerless.'

Jessica sighed. 'So that's what you meant earlier?'

The Prince nodded and replied, 'Yes.'

Bracken had a worried expression and said, 'Wonda told me powerful forces were upon us. Ooh... what if we fairies lose our ability to perform spells?'

Nomi sighed. 'I'm certain that won't happen.'

'Nothing is certain at a time like this,' said the Prince.

'Did Vienne tell you anything else about Surrain?' asked Laurel.

'No,' he replied.

'And what entity has rendered Vienne powerless? Was it the Grim Reaper?' asked Jessica.

The Prince sighed. 'Need I tell a sensitive soul like you, Jess?'

Jessica glanced at her friends and quietly replied, 'No. You're right.'

Prince Tal continued. 'When the three elf messengers told me the Grim Reaper had attacked them, I took no notice, even though I made a remark about their blue hair. We all know how the youngsters fantasize. I was more interested in the whereabouts of Surrain's letter.' The Prince sighed again. He leant over Surrain, kissed her cheek and whispered, 'I love you.'

The room was deadly silent and all eyes focused on Surrain. The little fairy didn't move a muscle. She lay perfectly still, in a tranquil state, as if she'd entered another world.

The appearance of the Grim Reaper and the other entities was a rare sight in the fairy kingdom and, contrary to popular belief, fairies are not immortal... they do die.

When a Faerie Funeral takes place, the ceremony is quite extraordinary. Fairies are elusive beings at the best of times, so few mortals have had the privilege of witnessing such a solemn occasion.

The fairy's body is wrapped in a shroud... Then at dawn, the individual is placed on hallowed ground at the foot of the Sacred Oak.

Fairies, elves, animals and birds gather round this great old tree and wait patiently for the soul of the dead to be released. After a short time a gentle breeze sweeps round the woods and the trees stir. Seconds later, dogs and wolves howl. Silence descends and the crowd watch closely. If the fairy has been good during her lifetime, the twinkling light of an angel appears and gently takes her soul to Forever Land; but if she's been a bad fairy, her soul is pulled out from her feet by evil soul collectors, and dragged down, down into the torments of Bolgus Bay, where she will endure eternal suffering. The body disappears from beneath the Sacred Oak...then the shroud ripples and fades away...

The Search

Nomi, Laurel, Bracken and Jessica made their way out of Surrain's bedroom, leaving Prince Tal alone with his thoughts. The four fairies didn't know what to do next, so they sat on the sofa yattering.

Meanwhile, Greega was still riding through the woods. As the Dog Man neared Surrain's cottage, a cold chill sent a shiver down his spine. Jameela sensed a ghostly presence and neighed loudly. As Greega looked around, he caught a glimpse of a cloaked figure standing next to his horse, under a canopy of trees. The Dog Guard thought his mind was playing tricks on him, so he pulled on Jameela's reins and brought her to a halt. Greega adjusted his eye patch and peered towards the trees. There, for sure, stood the solitary figure of doom, the Grim Reaper... His black horse stood proud, the silver armour covering his head and forelegs shimmered in the morning sun. Jameela felt intimidated by this great beast, more so, when his bloodshot eyes penetrated the essence of her soul. Jameela was raring to go, but the guard held her back. Greega glared at the gruesome pair. The jet-black horse eyeballed him. After a few daunting moments, the huge animal struck the sodden earth with his foreleg, and snorted flames from his wide nostrils.

Jameela struggled. She turned her head from side to side and stamped her foreleg into the ground. The golden horse was getting nowhere fast and she cried out in her husky voice, 'Greega, loosen the grip on my reins. We can't expose ourselves to this danger any longer.'

Greega patted Jameela, trying to reassure her. 'Don't fret, girl. The Grim Reaper isn't after us. Come on, we'd better make up for lost time.' And he whacked Jameela across the rump with his gauntlet.

Jameela was annoyed by his heavy handiness and yelled, 'Hey, Dog Man... That hurt. There's no need for violence. You're the hefty lummox getting a free ride here.'

Greega laughed, 'Hefty lummox eh? Well I'm no oaf. Now stop name-calling and be a good girlie.'

All of a sudden five soul collectors screeched overhead. The bickering pair, startled by these hooded entities, immediately stopped squabbling. Greega and Jameela felt uneasy and watched the evil beings disappear into the shadows. Greega loosened the reins and Jameela took off, galloping through the woods. Within minutes, Surrain's cottage was in sight. Jameela felt weary due to over-exertion. Not only was her load twice as heavy as usual, treading over soft damp ground had been difficult. The golden horse approached Surrain's gate and rested under the veranda.

The atmosphere was dismal. Greega dismounted and Jameela sighed with relief. The Dog Man marched past a crowd of creatures waiting for news and stomped into Surrain's cottage. The fairies were shocked by Greega's sudden arrival, more so when he rushed into Surrain's bedroom.

Prince Tal was appalled by Greega's untimely entrance. He jumped to his feet and shouted at the guard. 'Greega, what's possessed you to storm in here like this?'

'I'm sorry, Sir, this is vital. I must see if Surrain has any green lumps or blotches on the back of her neck.'

'This is most unexpected, Greega, and I'm surprised by your insistent request. Nevertheless, your intrusion tells me something is gravely wrong.'

Prince Tal perched on the left side of the bed. He gently moved Surrain's hair to the side and bared her neck, as Greega had demanded. The Prince couldn't believe his eyes and cried out, 'What the heck are those? Greega, do you know what's wrong with Surrain? I'm in desperate need of answers.'

The Dog Man stood back. He sighed deeply and replied, 'Sir, when Surrain's symptoms were described to me, I suspected she had eaten the green croag beetle. I'm sorry to say my suspicions have been confirmed. If only Surrain had eaten the orange croag beetle... she would be fine after experiencing short-term illusions.' Greega lowered his head. 'Sir, this is a solemn occasion. I believe Surrain ate the beetle three days ago and the green croag, no matter how small, is most deadly. Sadly there is little hope for Surrain. I'm so sorry.'

Nomi, Laurel, Bracken and Jessica stood listening by the open door. The fairies were more knowledgeable than the Prince regarding this insect, so when they heard Greega's comments they all gasped.

Nomi sat on the bed opposite Prince Tal and said, 'Poor Surrain. We can't give up on her now.'

'Who said anything about giving up?' cried the Prince.

Nomi sighed, 'I don't understand how Surrain could have eaten the poisonous insect. Green croag beetles live in toadstools and we only at mushrooms... so what's going on?'

Greega looked extremely sad. He nodded his head and replied, 'You're quite right Nomi. Croag beetles do live in toadstools. I recall a tragedy many years ago when six fairies died after celebrating. The fairies in question met in the woods and, according to tradition, they gathered mushrooms; but some green speckled toadstools were accidentally mixed in with the pile. I'm afraid that's the only explanation for this too.'

Jessica cried out, 'There must be something we can do.'

'An anti-dote... that's what we need!' exclaimed Laurel.

'Of course,' replied the Prince, and he looked straight at Greega. 'Is there anything that will neutralize the poison?' Before the guard had time to answer, Prince Tal asked another question. 'Greega, what do you know about this insect?'

'Well, Sir, Crogan, one of the first mortals in the land, discovered the beetle. This was after a number of animals died in suspicious circumstances. Crogan performed a post-mortem examination on each creature and was flabbergasted by his findings. Every animal was riddled with tiny green insects. Crogan had a theory, so he combed the forest where the dead animals were found and searched for green beetles. On his way home, the scientist stumbled across orange speckled toadstools. He was intrigued by this new fungus and took a few samples back to his laboratory. On closer inspection, these orange speckled toadstools were found to have beetles of the same colour, living on their undersides. Not only were the orange beetles similar to the green beetles... they were the same species. Crogan was delighted, now he could start experimenting. After a period of trial and error, Crogan had a breakthrough. Fluid from the orange insect proved to be a successful anti-dote for the animals that had eaten the poisonous green beetle.'

The Prince was really surprised by Greega's knowledge. He said, 'Mm. As you are so well informed, Greega, I want more details. How can we acquire the anti-dote?'

Greega was a little reluctant to divulge this information and he hesitated. 'Erm...'

'Out with it Greega.... We're in a sorry situation here.'

'Of course, Sir, it's just...' Greega sighed. 'I don't know if the anti-dote will work on Surrain. Besides, it's vital that the correct measure is diluted.'

The Prince was becoming more edgy by the second. He stood up, stared at Greega and shouted, 'Surely Crogan documented his findings. Do you know if any such papers exist?'

'Yes Sir, there are two volumes in the library...and I have read some of his work.'

'There are two volumes? Ooh, Greega, we've no time to go through that amount of material now. Tell me everything you know... and I mean everything,' demanded the Prince.

Greega disclosed the information, making sure his activities in the dungeon remained a secret.

'Sir, the orange fluid has two uses, one for an anti-dote and the other can be taken as a drink. On the odd occasion, I myself have used fluid from the orange croag beetle. Droplets are diluted in water and Crogan called the juice Halloopigoo. Apparently, the symptoms of those who drink halloopigoo are much the same as those who have eaten the green croag beetle. Their mental condition changes... they appear to be a little loopy and experience similar hallucinations, hence the name, halloopigoo. The substance takes an hour or so to get into the bloodstream and wears off a couple of hours later. Sir, even though Surrain experienced hallucinations, we have proof she ate the green croag beetle during her party. And regarding the anti-dote, it's usually administered within twenty four hours to be effective.' Greega shook his head and sighed deeply whilst looking at Surrain.

Prince Tal wasn't deterred by Greega's gloomy outlook. He sat on the edge of the bed and said, 'It's a matter of life and death, so I'll try anything at this stage. Greega, search the woods for orange beetles. When you've found what you think is an adequate amount, extract the substance.' Then the Prince glanced at the fairies, 'Who will join Greega and seek out the orange croag beetles?'

Laurel instantly volunteered. Being Keeper of Dreams, Laurel believed she could make contact with Surrain, but she kept this to herself. 'Greega, we'll leave at once,' she said.

Within seconds Laurel and Greega had vanished.

Meanwhile, word about Surrain's illness was spreading. Roster flew to Magentis Castle. He asked the sorceress to help Surrain, but soon found out she was powerless. Vienne told Roster to visit Tamzin and Taneesha, and explain the situation to them. Then the fairies were to go straight to Magentis Castle, inform Meidi and take him to the south tower. Vienne stressed that time was of the essence.

The owl's work was soon completed. The peach-haired sisters promptly vanished and appeared inside Magentis Castle. First stop was the Grand Master's chambers. When Taneesha told Meidi the bad news about Surrain, he smirked, which was most unexpected. Tamzin and Taneesha were annoyed by Meidi's shameful response. As requested, the fairies took him to the south tower. Vienne welcomed the two fairies. She gave them an account of her vision, while Meidi stood around looking uncomfortable. The Grand Master resented the company he was keeping, especially the fairies. Their capabilities were more than a threat. Meidi wanted to return to his chambers, but, being ruler of the kingdom, he knew it was his duty to visit Surrain, so he gritted his teeth and kept quiet. Tamzin uttered a spell. The two fairies, along with Vidor, Vienne and Meidi appeared in Surrain's garden. By now the crowd had increased, and whilst awaiting news, they talked quietly amongst themselves.

Back in the forest, Laurel and Greega were standing in the area thick with orange speckled toadstools. Greega knew exactly where to find this fungi and he told Laurel sometime earlier. They both picked toadstools, taking the beetles from the underside. Then Greega extracted the fluid, saving the droplets in a phial.

'I'm sure this amount will be sufficient,' said the Dog Man.

'All right Greega. I'll get you back straight away... just relax,' said Laurel.

No sooner had Greega taken a breath in, when he shuddered and materialized inside Surrain's home. Greega appeared alone, as Laurel had other ideas. The guard diluted the fluid with a drop of water and made his way to the bedroom. No-one noticed Laurel's absence, as all eyes were focused on Surrain. Then Greega injected the serum into Surrain's arm. Prince Tal and the fairies were full of expectations. Bracken nipped outside to tell the crowd... now all they could do was hope and pray.

During this time, Laurel had appeared in her own cottage. The fair-haired fairy knew exactly where she was going to go. Being keeper of dreams, there was only one place. Laurel lay on her bed and drifted through dreams into the Realm of Isk-us-barooska. Laurel expected to see Surrain, so she could encourage the little fairy to fight her illness and regain consciousness, although her findings were somewhat disturbing.

'I'm not giving up. There's still hope,' said Laurel. And she returned to Surrain's cottage.

Laurel arrived to hear a chorus of howling wolves and dogs... her deepest fears had come true.

Dark clouds floated over Surrain's cottage and tears filled everyone's eyes but Meidi's.

Prince Tal, Greega and the fairies watched helplessly, as Surrain, Faerie of the Forest, began to slip away.

A Significant Journey

A dark heaviness hovered over the Kingdom of Deyn. Only the Grand Master hoped the little fairy would pass away, making his cunning plan that much easier.

Greega walked up to Prince Tal and stood beside Surrain's bed. The guard pulled off his gauntlet. Greega held the little fairy's limp wrist and took her pulse. The guard had a sorrowful look. He glanced at the Prince and said, 'Sir, Surrain's pulse is very weak. I'm sorry to say, the anti-dote has failed. Surrain is hanging on by a thread.'

During this time Surrain was experiencing an altered state of euphoria. Earlier that day, she had entered the dream Realm of Isk-us-barooska, where Kirrey welcomed her with open arms. The little fairy woke up momentarily, smiled at Prince Tal and closed her eyes. Surrain returned to Isk-us-barooska and a peaceful tranquillity began to fill her soul.

Laurel entered the Realm of Isk-us-barooska at the precise moment Surrain reached the tunnel of light. Laurel knew there was nothing she could do. Surrain had become wrapped up in Kirrey's love and the angel had enveloped her. Surrain and Kirrey hovered beneath the brightly lit tunnel, where a fine mist and a soft wind encircled them. As their long white gowns flowed in the gentle breeze, Surrain leant back gracefully. The little fairy gazed into Kirrey's deep blue eyes. Surrain was captivated by his devoted charm and they smiled endearingly at one another.

Surrain, whose spirit was reaching towards Forever Land, looked down at her motionless body. The only way she could communicate with her loved ones, was through one of her poems. All of a sudden, Surrain's book of poetry flew into her bedroom and landed on her quilt. Prince Tal and the whole group jumped back with surprise. The onlookers watched as the book opened wide, the pages flicking one way, then the other, before falling open on Surrain's last poem, titled 'Letting Go.' Golden stars fluttered down, and fell onto the book, disappearing into the rhyme. This poem was familiar to the fairies as they had read it earlier, and they looked horrified. Prince Tal picked up the book and walked out of the room, sighing as he re-read the first verse of the poem over and over.

> 'In the Kingdom of Deyn, the land where we met,
> Our time together I'll never forget.
> I feel tired and weary I just want to rest,
> Now I know... this life is a test.'

Meanwhile, Surrain felt safe, happy and protected in Kirrey's arms. Surrain and Kirrey watched from above as more creatures of the wood gathered round the cottage.

The lingering presence in Surrain's home lifted. Outside there were no dark clouds... the sky was blue. Warmth from the sun shone down and heat replaced the cold chill that once filled the air.

Prince Tal left Surrain's cottage in disbelief, holding Surrain's book close to his chest. He looked straight at Vidor who, for some strange reason, was smiling. The Prince felt a mixture of emotions and cried out, 'This is ridiculous. We live in a magical land and we cannot save Surrain.'

Vidor rubbed his hands together and said, 'Don't give up yet.'

Vienne glanced at the Prince. Then she gazed at her clenched fists. 'Look at this blue glow surrounding my hands. When the dark clouds drifted by, my powers returned like a surge of electricity running through my veins. I will bring Surrain back. Wait and see.'

Vienne and Vidor headed for Surrain's bedroom. The pair stood at either side of the bed, while the fairies, Meidi and Greega moved back. Prince Tal entered the room and stood by the door.

Vienne breathed deeply and cried out, 'I've been charged with energy like never before. I'm going to put an end to this misery and bring Surrain back to where she belongs.'

The sorceress proceeded. She took two crystals from her pocket, rubbed them together and uttered,

> 'Oh beautiful green emerald and magnificent zircon,
> Your healing powers I call upon.
> Work your magic... bring back Surrain,
> Let the Kingdom of Deyn feel happiness again.'

Spectators outside Surrain's cottage could see flickering lights coming from inside her bedroom. Suddenly, a lightning bolt struck the forest floor sending shock waves along the ground. The violence unnerved the onlookers. Nevertheless, they stood fast, waiting for results.

Surrain was in a calm and tranquil state. Then she felt a sudden pull on her body. The little fairy held tightly to Kirrey, but the force was too strong. Surrain was being torn away from the veil of love that surrounded her. As the power from Vienne gradually drew Surrain's spirit back to the land of the living, Kirrey lost his grip. Surrain and Kirrey's hands were finally pulled apart... and they were separated. With outstretched arms, Surrain and Kirrey tried desperately to reach each other. Surrain sobbed as she found herself being drawn back, down the tunnel of light. She called out to Kirrey, who was unable to respond. Kirrey could not prevent the suction-like pull that intensified, and he watched in dismay as Surrain fell further away from him. As the little fairy descended towards Isk-us-barooska, a feeling of emptiness enveloped her and she uttered a piercing cry.

Meanwhile, the sorceress had used an excessive amount of energy trying to revive Surrain.

Vienne stepped away from Surrain's bedside and said, 'It's no use, Vidor, I can't continue.'

The magician bit his lip. In frustration he cried out, 'Vienne. Don't give up!'

The sorceress sighed. She looked at Vidor sympathetically and said, 'You've got to accept that Surrain has gone to a better place... perhaps a place where she's needed.'

'She's needed here. Look around you, woman. Veela and Sovran have crept under the bed feeling dejected. And there's a forest of creatures out there, waiting for Surrain to recover.'

Vienne's impatience with her husband was growing. She lifted her arms in the air and yelled, 'Ooh, Vidor, I give up with you sometimes.'

The magician didn't like Vienne's reply and he raised his voice even more, 'Huh, if that's your attitude, I'll try to revive Surrain!'

The sorceress scowled at Vidor and shouted, 'You're not a miracle worker, you know.'

'No, I'm a magician, and a splendid one at that. I have powers that are expected of me in times like these.' Vidor gritted his teeth. Then he stared at his wife and said, 'You know, Vienne, you can be so patronizing.'

Vienne ignored Vidor's remark and, due to the circumstances, everyone felt uneasy.

Prince Tal was grief-stricken. He'd had enough of their arguing and sat on the sofa in the living room. Greega also walked out of the bedroom and made his way outside. The Dog Man stood quietly beside Sian, Feebee, Tamzin, Taneesha, the three elves, the dogs and Jameela.

Meanwhile, Nomi, Laurel, Bracken and Jessica were shocked. They stayed huddled together in the bedroom.

The sorceress joined Prince Tal and sat next to him. Without saying a word, the Prince gave Vienne Surrain's little book of poetry. Vienne flicked through the pages and stopped at Surrain's last poem, titled, 'Letting go.'

Vienne read the poem and a moment later she spoke directly to her husband. 'I'm sorry to say this, Vidor, but where did you get splendid from? Your forte is trickery and illusion... that won't bring Surrain back. If my brother was here, instead of attending every Witches Assembly in the universe, it would be a different story. Now turn your eyes to this rhyme...proof of Surrain's passing.'

Vidor shook his head in denial and walked outside. As soon as the crowd saw the magician's face, they knew it was bad news. There were murmurs and many decided to go home. The sad news swept through the woods like wildfire. The carpet of colour that filled the land, turned into sorrowful wilting blooms and a strange sense of calm befell the fairy kingdom.

Prince Tal's anguish was clear to see. He looked at Vienne and said, 'I suppose your way of dealing with grief is picking on Vidor?'

The sorceress tapped the Prince on his knee and replied, 'You're right. But he does annoy me at times. Oh, Tal, I'm so sorry about Surrain.'

Roster flew down from Surrain's roof and perched on the garden gate. The owl wouldn't accept Surrain's passing and he, along with a few others, waited in hope.

Although Vienne had given up on Surrain, the little fairy continued her descent. The tunnel of light seemed never ending. Suddenly, Kirrey grabbed hold of Surrain. As she clutched Kirrey's gown, Surrain felt a combination of feelings and cried out, 'Kirrey, I don't know if I'm coming or going. What's happening? Why am I being pushed back and forth? Everything felt calm until we were forced apart.'

Kirrey comforted Surrain and her distress lifted. The angel spoke softly and said, 'Let me explain why you have been thrown into disarray. The sorceress tried to revive you, although her dabbling has had little effect. The Supreme Force that controls our destiny, the One who knows our every thought and deed, has intervened. This intervention coincided with Vienne's magic. Remember how you came to be in this situation? You were celebrating your happiness. During the feasting, you accidentally ate a poisonous beetle. Surrain, you should not be here...this is not your time. After a significant journey, you will return to the ones you love and the kingdom you cherish.'

Surrain reached up, cupping Kirrey's face in her hands. Then, with a look of despair, she stared into his eyes and pleaded with him, 'Kirrey, I want to stay here with you...Please. The feeling of peace and tranquillity is overwhelming. Please, Kirrey... Please! I can watch over my loved ones and be with you at the same time.'

Kirrey had an air of sadness about him and he drew Surrain closer. 'What you say is true, but that is not the issue here. You are not listening to me, Surrain... I have no choice in the matter. I've been told that this is Not your time. Surrain, when we were pulled apart and you descended, the sensation of losing you caused me pain, the hurt of which I've never experienced before. It made me realise how your loved ones must feel. Surrain, go, and be happy. I won't be losing you, for when you drift through dreams into the Realm of Isk-us-barooska, I will be there waiting. I can take you way beyond anything you could imagine, where anything is possible. Surrain, together we will visit places that are never ending. So return to your Prince, who loves you dearly. There are many years of happiness ahead for you both.'

Surrain snuggled into Kirrey and held on tighter than ever. She was clearly distraught and sobbed, 'Kirrey, I can't let go. I don't want to break free. You fill my thoughts and mind endlessly.'

Kirrey leaned back and faced Surrain. He gazed into her eyes and whispered, 'I really love you.'

As Surrain stared into his deep blue eyes, tears rolled down her cheeks. 'My darling, Kirrey, I see you as never before. It is only now I realise... you are the mirror of my soul.'

Kirrey held Surrain as close as he could, softly whispering in her ear, 'I cannot prevent this turmoil you are enduring. If only I could stop it and whisk you away.'

A few seconds of silence swept by as Kirrey and Surrain held each other. Everything was happening so fast and within moments Surrain felt another pull against her body.

Kirrey whispered, 'Surrain, shortly you will be entering the Realm of Isk-us-barooska. You will be in a dream state. Then, with a little help from me, you will regain consciousness.'

All of a sudden an unseen power penetrated the couple. Surrain became separated from Kirrey. Once again the little fairy cried out to her Guardian Angel. Surrain rolled forward. Then she was dragged backwards through a sea of mist. Surrain was in mid-air and as she struggled to turn, she could feel tremendous heat rising from below. Surrain extended her arms and found she was flying above a haunting and chaotic world. Trapped souls consumed by the torment of Hell-Fire, were trying in vain, to escape. Their cries of pain and misery terrified Surrain. Then the little fairy was drawn into a narrow tunnel. The light was dim and a warm breeze swept around her. She could see a bluish glow just ahead. As she approached the end of the tunnel, the echoes of sadness faded. There, on a sea of clouds, Surrain was able to stand up and view her surroundings. It was a silent and calm atmosphere... a world between worlds where dimness and emptiness encompassed her. As Surrain looked around, she became overcome with fear. Feeling lost and alone, Surrain cried out in despair.

'Kirrey... Kir-rey! Where are you? Kirrey... have you forsaken me?'

Surrain's Guardian Angel suddenly appeared. He stood at arms length from Surrain and took hold of her shoulders. Then Kirrey gazed into Surrain's tear-filled eyes with deep affection and said, 'My love is like no other, comparable to none... although Prince Tal being a Draemid comes close. My dear Surrain, with all the love I feel, how could I ever abandon you? I will be here to watch over you, guide and protect you, until you day is nigh. The Divine force that penetrated us, would not allow my presence to accompany you through your emotional return. And now you are almost there. Surrain, you are an exceptional fairy, who has had a unique experience. When you wake-up and feel ready, I want you to turn to the very last page in your book of poems.'

Surrain instantly calmed down. Even though the little fairy looked puzzled, she felt an air of excitement.

All of a sudden nothing else mattered. Kirrey stared at Surrain with intensity and she could feel his eyes penetrating her soul. This gave Surrain a nice, but nervous sensation in her stomach. Kirrey wrapped his arms round Surrain. As they were encased in a cocoon-like protection, their lips touched. It was a magical moment of unexpected passion that melted Surrain's heart...one she would not forget. Then Kirrey breathed into the little fairy and she slowly revived.

The little fairy heard Kirrey say, 'Listen carefully Surrain. Breathe deeply and remember... I will always be here for you. Live your life and let everyone think it was the sorceress who brought you back into being. Only we shall know the truth. Now... open your eyes.'

This time Surrain smiled and Kirrey faded into the distance. And without question, Surrain returned to the land of the living.

The Awakening

Surrain's motionless body suddenly jolted. The little fairy lay still for a few more moments. Nomi, Laurel, Bracken and Jessica didn't notice. The fairies were engrossed in their conversation, yattering about the good times. Prince Tal sat in the other room with his head in his hands. Moments later the Prince sighed and looked across at Meidi. The Grand Master seemed to be lacking any emotion, making himself quite comfortable in Surrain's fireside chair and staring into the fire.

'How can this be, Meidi? You clearly stated that Surrain and I were meant to be together.'

Meidi replied abruptly, without any hesitation. 'I only repeated what the sorceress told me.'

Suddenly, giggles were heard coming from Surrain's bedroom. Prince Tal leapt from his seat and rushed into the room. Vidor and Vienne joined the Prince, along with Meidi, Sian, Fee, Tamzin and Taneesha. The group found Surrain sitting up chuckling with Veela and Sovran who were nuzzling into her. Everyone expressed their happiness...everyone except Meidi. Inwardly, the two-faced ruler was seething with anger at Surrain's recovery and he tried hard not to show his ill-feeling.

Meidi's face grew redder by the second, until his blood vessels looked like bursting. Then, in a frenzied rage, he snarled at Veela and Sovran, yelling, 'Get off the bed. Get out!'

The wolves growled and jumped down, joining Becky, Orfeo and Reah outside.

Surrain's visitors were taken aback by Meidi's offensive attitude. For the time being, nothing was said... No-one wanted to cause a scene and spoil Prince Tal's moment with Surrain.

The Prince sat close to Surrain and whispered, 'It's good to have you back. Only minutes ago we thought we'd lost you.'

As Prince Tal held Surrain's hand, she replied, 'It's good to be back.'

Surrain was pale-faced and drawn. The little fairy looked weary, as if she'd endured a long and tiring journey. As Surrain inched herself up the bed, she said, 'I'm really thirsty. Could I have a glass of water please?'

Laurel uttered a spell and the jug filled with water. She poured a glass and passed it to Surrain. Meanwhile, Nomi, Bracken, Jessica, Sian, Fee, Tamzin and Taneesha stood by the end of the bed. The fairies kept a close eye on Meidi, whose outlandish behaviour baffled them.

All of a sudden the Grand Master was overcome with joy. Meidi startled everyone, when he threw his arms in the air and cried out, 'Oh Praise Be! The wonder of the sorceress has worked after all.'

Meidi's actions came out of the blue and this made the fairies more suspicious.

Prince Tal was preoccupied with Surrain. Nevertheless, he reminded everyone of what the guard had done. 'Let's not forget Greega. He's the one who diagnosed Surrain's illness and returned with the anti-dote.'

Roster was perched on the windowsill, squawking with delight. 'Surrain has recovered... I knew it, I knew it! I'll spread the word. I'll let all and sundry know Surrain, Faerie of the Forest, is as well as can be.'

Vidor smiled and shouted, 'Go on Roster. Spread your wings and fly... enlighten them all.'

The owl took to the air and screeched loudly, alerting the forest creatures. 'I have good news. Hurry to the woodcutter's yard, and I'll spread glad tidings.'

The array of animals wasted no time and rushed through the woods. Meanwhile, Roster headed towards Magentis Castle to inform the others.

Creatures were skipping and chirping birds were flying round every cottage in the area. Then the animals and birds approached a misty area, surrounding the old crones' shack.

Ibsis and Igfreid were having a party of their own...slurping wine and belching as they celebrated Surrain's death. When the old crones heard all the commotion outside, their curiosity was roused.

After burping and breaking wind, Igfreid yelled at her sister, 'Move your fat butt, Ibsis. Take a look and see what's going on.'

Ibsis scrambled to her feet. The old crone peered round the curtains and rubbed the grubby glass. She screwed her face up and scowled at the creatures rushing across her land. Then Ibsis cried out as she flung the curtains together, 'Animals are everywhere. Quick Igfreid, look in your crystal ball. We'll soon find out what's happening.'

The sisters gazed into their cloudy crystals. After a few seconds, a look of horror swept across their wrinkled faces.

Ibsis began to wail. In a fit of temper, she ripped the hair band out of her pony-tail and threw it across the room. She sat down and sobbed whilst banging both fists on the tabletop.

Two candlesticks fell to the floor and Igfreid grabbed the crystal balls, tankards and jug of wine. 'Ibsis, please take control.'

Suddenly Ibsis leapt from her chair. She jumped up and down with clenched fists, screaming like a lunatic. 'How can I take control? The forest was mine! Mine I say... until that poodle-top opened her eyes. Why? Oh W-h-y...?'

Igfreid, the more laid back of the two, tried talking sense to her sister, but she was fighting a losing battle. 'Calm down, Ibsis. I'm sure it will be all right.'

Ibsis glared at her sibling and screeched, 'All right? No, Igfreid, it won't be all right. Stop talking piffle. Surrain's been in the way far too long now. Ooh no, I've just had an awful thought... or maybe it's a premonition. Do you know what, Igfreid? She'll be a Fairy Queen next.'

'I very much doubt that, Ibsis. Surrain's already got a title being lover of the woods an' all.'

Ibsis sniggered. 'You're forgetting something, dear sister. There was no official announcement. Surrain is only known as Faerie of the Forest. But if she dares to marry our Prince, then her title will be official.' Ibsis thought for a few moments. As her mind worked overtime, she twisted her face, distorting her rough and ready appearance. 'Mm. Something interesting has just occurred to me. If a title is bestowed upon Surrain, once she's in Isk-us-barooska, she won't be able resist having a nosy and going to the Realm of Elfina in Zenith... Then, after her third visit she'll be trapped there. I'll whisper sweet nothings in Meidi's ear and encourage him to give that blonde poodle-top a title. When we have a Fairy Queen, we'll soon be rid of her... just like the others. He he heee...'

Igfreid chuckled and replied, 'Ooh, Ibsis, you are a crafty one. That's good thinking on your part. We'll just have Andreen and her clan to deal with. He he he, how exciting...'

Ibsis sighed. Her mood had changed dramatically and she sat beside Igfreid rubbing her hands together. Then Ibsis grinned, exposing a few of her black stumpy teeth. 'Those two kids and that so-called magician will be no problem. It's the sorceress and that twin brother of hers, who'll cause us difficulty.'

The sisters gazed into their crystal balls. As cloudy images appeared, the sniggering pair continued to stuff their faces, whilst consuming large amounts of their home brew.

Meanwhile, animals and birds were congregating in the woodcutter's yard. Roster arrived and perched on a wooden fence. He waved his wings inwardly, beckoning the creatures. 'Gather round, gather round,' he cried.

Roster disturbed the woodpile five. The mice were sheltering under a heap of logs, and popped their heads out of small crevices. To their surprise, they saw a number of animals meeting in the yard. They scurried along the wood and stood on top of the pile, waiting to hear Roster's news.

Jud the woodcutter heard all the commotion and watched the goings on from an open window in his cottage.

Meanwhile, Jack and Sebbi sat at the kitchen table, fiddling with their long green beards.

Suddenly, a black cockerel uttered his characteristic cry, 'Cock a doodle do! Cock a doodle doo!'

The owl's eyes widened. As Roster stared at the large crowing bird, his anger was building up. Then he shouted, 'Hey, Cocky...Stop crowing. Shut your beak and listen to me. I've got an announcement to make!'

The cockerel ignored Roster...this was his territory, so he continued to crow.

Roster stretched out his wings and yelled, 'Fox! Hey, Mr Fox!'

The big red fox looked straight at Roster. He pointed to himself and mouthed the word, 'Me?'

Roster let out a deep sigh and muttered, 'Ooh who else?' A moment later he yelled, 'Yes, you! Do you see that crowing beak?'

The fox stood on his hind legs and glanced over the crowd. He smiled and nodded at Roster.

'Well, smack him in the gob! That blustering bird's had all morning to crow.'

Three fox cubs jumped for joy and everyone heard their squeaky voices crying out, 'Dad... Dad! Can we get him? Or do you want to lamp him one yourself?'

The old fox leant down and whispered to his youngsters. Then he stood upright with a big grin spreading across his face. A couple of seconds later, the dog fox swaggered across to the crowing bird, took a swing and walloped the unsuspecting cockerel.

The stunned bird collapsed to the ground. Everyone gasped. After a moment, the cockerel opened one eye... then the other. He'd been knocked cross-eyed by the blow. The cockerel had double vision and gazed at two smirking images of Mr Fox. In a high pitched cry he squealed, 'I'm shocked by such unruly conduct.' As he picked himself up, his head veered from side to side and he gave Roster a foul look.

In return, Roster squawked, 'Next time chicken, shut your beak and listen. Don't be a cocksure ignoramus.'

Dazed by his thrashing, the cockerel stomped off towards the hen house, followed by his clucking brood.

Roster sighed. 'Right, I'll continue. As most of you are aware, earlier today, Faerie of the Forest passed into Forever Land. But I'm telling you now... that is Not the case! I'm here to bring glad tidings. It's splendid news... Splendid! Surrain is indeed alive and well...so go, spread the news!'

Everyone applauded and the sweet melody of bird song began to sweep through the woods.

The creatures scattered and Roster took to the air. The owl looked down and saw masses of flowers opening up producing carpets of blooms. Then he saw Jessica's younger brother sitting beneath a tree. The white owl flew towards Tomar and screeched, 'Hey you... banana top! Why do you look so miserable?'

Tomar sat weeping. He shaded his bloodshot eyes from the beaming sun and watched Roster land on a nearby tree stump. The snivelling youngster bawled, 'Goodness me, Roster, have you no feelings? Why are you making so much noise when most creatures are undercover grieving? And for your information, my t-shirt is lemon.'

'All right... so it's lemon. Tomar, I've got a good reason for being here.'

Roster's words fell on deaf ears and the little elf continued talking. 'I'm upset about Surrain and I don't want you squawking nonsense down my ear. Will you go away and let me mourn alone?'

'No I will not go away!' exclaimed Roster. 'Tomar, I'm trying to tell you something. Let me get a word in edgeways, you little tyke.'

The puzzled youngster stopped crying. He walked up to Roster and said, 'I've not seen you behave like this before. You're really bringing attention to yourself. What's up?'

Roster was becoming flustered. The white owl stretched his wings and sighed as he gazed into the sky. 'Ooh question after question. Now be q-u-i-e-t! My patience is wearing very thin. Listen up, boy. Surrain is alive and well. So I'm spreading the good news. OK?'

Just at that moment, a swarm of bees flew overhead. Their tiny furry bodies formed the word 'Hooray' then they took off.

Tomar smiled and Roster said, 'See. I've enlightened the creatures of the forest and once again it's buzzing with activity. Those bees are going to create a lavish performance above Surrain's cottage. It'll be a splendid display. Now be off with you, Tomar.'

The young elf cheered up no-end and toddled off home, singing along with the birds.

Roster's episode with Tomar was exhausting, so he stayed on the tree stump until he'd calmed down.

During this time, well-wishers popped in and out of Surrain's bedroom. They noticed the little fairy had a thirst like never before, drinking water by the jug full. The clear liquid gave Surrain a much needed boost, but the effect on her weak body soon came to light.

Then Dayar, Ryar and L.J. peered round the door.

Surrain saw their cheeky faces and blue hair. The little fairy smiled and beckoned the trio. 'Come in and sit here,' she said patting her duvet. 'And how are my favourite messengers today?'

Each elf gave Surrain a big hug and kiss, before making themselves comfortable on her bed.

L.J. was really excited. The young elf had lots to tell Surrain, but he didn't know where to begin. 'We're so glad you're back with us, Surrain,' he cried out. 'We saw the Grim Reaper and I thought he had taken you away. I don't know what would happen to us and our forest without you.'

Surrain smiled and held the youngsters hand. 'Life goes on, L.J. Sooner or later we all have to make that special journey into the unknown. I just hope when my turn comes, you all continue my work, helping the animals. They need love and support from us, especially as we are their guardians. And what's this I hear, L.J.? At last the elixir has worked.'

L.J. lowered his head and giggled along with Dayar and Ryar.

Then loud clumpy footsteps were heard. Deadly silence filled the room. As the footsteps continued to approach, all heads turned towards the door. The loud tread suddenly stopped. Tension was building. In the suspense, everyone stared wide-eyed, watching and waiting with bated-breath. All of a sudden, Greega popped his head round the door.

Sighs of relief were uttered.

Surrain quietly said, 'Oh, Greega, for a moment you had us all going. It's great to see you. Come on in.'

The Dog Guard walked towards Surrain and smiled. 'I'm glad to see you looking well. Jameela and I were on our way back to Magentis Castle when Roster stopped us. He was squawking for joy and told us Vienne's magic had worked after all. You know me though... I had to see you for myself.'

Surrain looked at Greega with affection. She tilted her head and said, 'Greega, thank you so much for helping. When you injected me, I could see my body from afar. It was weird being an observer from above, and I want to express my gratitude to you all.'

Surrain's visitors seemed a little uncomfortable. No-one knew what to say, so Prince Tal broke the silence.

'Mm,' uttered the Prince. 'Now, on the subject of halloopigoo... With regard to this intoxicating substance and Greega's exceptional knowledge, considering the circumstances, I will turn a blind eye.'

Greega was vexed. The guard grunted, stepped back and pawed at his eye patch.

Prince Tal suddenly realised what he had said. The Prince jumped up and grabbed the guard's arm, apologising. 'Greega, I'm sorry. Please don't take offence. You know I didn't mean any disrespect. I forgot Dog Men don't have the same sense of humour as us. Just put that comment behind you.'

Greega adjusted his eye patch and nodded in reply.

Prince Tal wasn't as subtle as Surrain, who changed the subject to relieve the tension.

'Hopefully, after the social gathering, the next get-together will be a great celebration,' said Surrain, gazing at Prince Tal.

The Prince kissed Surrain on her cheek and replied, 'That's right. When you're feeling well enough, we'll plan our wedding... the sooner the better.'

Before another word was spoken, a dark cloud floated over the cottage. Murmurs were heard amongst Surrain's visitors, who made their way towards the windows.

Suddenly, an incredible sight unfolded before their very eyes. Surrain and Prince Tal were able to see the event without moving from their places. They, along with the spectators, watched in awe as millions of bees spelled out the following message.

'To our Honey...Faerie of the Forest...Get well soon.'

Surrain smiled and said, 'Aw...that's delightful.'

When the show was over, Surrain's visitors returned to her bedside.

The little fairy looked noticeably tired, so Nomi decided to make the first move. 'We should leave Surrain in peace. She needs a good rest to recuperate.' Nomi glanced at Meidi and Greega. 'Do you want to get back to Magentis Castle in an instant?'

'I'd appreciate that,' replied Greega.

'So would I,' added Meidi, and he shuffled towards Surrain. 'I wish you well. Have a quick recovery.'

Greega suddenly raised his voice. 'What about Jameela? She's outside.'

'There's no need to worry,' said the Prince. 'Jameela can go along with you and the fairies.'

Vidor tapped Prince Tal on the back. 'We're off too, my boy.' The magician smiled and placed his arm round Vienne's waist. 'Come on, dear, they need some time alone. Shortly, we'll be having the social gathering and soon after that event, we'll be merrymaking at the wedding of this exceptional pair. Something we can look forward too.'

The sorceress snuggled into her husband and replied, 'Yes, Vidor, at last I agree with you.' The couple said their goodbyes and left the bedroom. Just then, Andreen and Rew entered the cottage. The youngsters had the foxywuffs in tow and Vienne said, 'Surrain is doing fine. She's had enough well-wishers for today, so come on... we'll go home together.' There was no argument and in a short space of time the family had vanished.

Nomi leaned across to Surrain and kissed her on the cheek. 'We're leaving too. We'll pop in tomorrow to see how you are feeling.'

Tamzin and Taneesha waved to Surrain from the bedroom door.

Then Dayar called out to the fairies, startling everyone. 'I hope you don't think I'm being cheeky, but could you get us home in an instant too? It's nearly meal-time and our stomachs are rumbling.'

Laughter filled the room.

'Typical,' said Bracken. 'Trust you elves to be thinking about food. Let's go outside.'

Dayar, Ryar and L.J. waved goodbye to Surrain. This left Prince Tal, Surrain and Greega in the room.

The Dog Man stood at the end of the bed and smiled at the little fairy. 'Good luck, Surrain. Hope to see you soon in the courtyard.' Greega promptly joined the others, while Veela and Sovran crept into Surrain's bedroom.

Laurel was already outside, trying to arrange the crowd leaving with the fairies. 'Right... Because there are so many of us, I want the animals in the centre of the circle. Not you, Spicklebud. Prickly Urchin House is just across the way.' By now Laurel was becoming flustered. 'No, Greega... I mean the dogs and Jameela inside the circle. You're a bit different. Stand between Tam and Taneesha.' Then Laurel noticed Spicklebud plod off miserably. A feeling of guilt enveloped Laurel. As the old hog whipped out his handkerchief and blew his nose trumpet style, Laurel called out to him, 'Spicklebud, I'm sorry. Come back and join the others in the circle.'

Meanwhile, Veela and Sovran were watching the goings on through the picture window in Surrain's bedroom.

Bracken cried out, 'Laurel, I'll do the honours. Everyone seems to be in place. So, are we ready?'

As the crowd nodded in reply, grunts, murmurs and other strange noises were heard.

Once again the plum-haired fairy glanced round the group. After a moment, Bracken whispered the appropriate spell, and they were gone.

A Draemid Secret Revealed

Surrain's well-wishers finally departed and Prince Tal sighed with relief. He closed the bedroom door and sat in the bedside chair.

'At last, it's just the two of us,' he said, smiling at Surrain.

Veela and Sovran didn't like that remark. They walked towards Surrain and made deep guttural sounds, reminding the Prince of their presence.

Prince Tal tutted, 'OK... It's the four of us. Now go over there,' he cried out, shooing them away.

Veela was visibly irritated by Prince Tal's dominance and made her feelings clear. 'Well if that's your attitude, we'll go back outside and sit in the sunshine. Come along, Sovran.'

'Whatever,' said the Prince... he rose to his feet and opened the front door.

Surrain chuckled. 'What a performance from Veela. She can be dramatic at times, just like Becky.'

Prince Tal sighed and said, 'Surrain, you look really tired. Do you want me to leave you in peace so you can sleep?'

'No, not just yet... I fancy having a chat, a kind of heart to heart.'

'All right, what's on your mind?'

'Well, something has been puzzling me about your people. You know... the Tekwah's People of the Draemid Nation.'

The Prince folded his arms and said, 'Mm... sounds ominous.'

'No, it's nothing to worry about. It's more like curiosity on my part.'

'Fire away then.'

Surrain sat comfortably and began. 'When I travelled through the vortex and met Taz, she introduced me to other Draemids. I soon realised they could read my thoughts and I found that invasion of privacy hard to accept. Anyway, here in this kingdom, neither of you have that ability unless it's with another Draemid. Why?'

'It's strange really,' replied the Prince. After a sigh, he continued. 'Telepathy fails me in regard to the inhabitants of this land. As you know, I've met two Draemids in this kingdom and thought communication has flowed between us, Taz was one, the other was Tithe. I met Tithe some years ago in Meidi's chambers. When my eyes set upon him, I knew instinctively he was a very close relative, and a Draemid from Drakohsia. Only then did I realise what I was capable of. But when I visit the outside world, there is no way I can use telepathy.'

'Interesting... Now tell me... why shouldn't the mortal population know the truth about your background?'

'Why indeed? I'm sure it's to do with a promise or a pact made in the past. Anyway, what does it matter?'

'I suppose it doesn't,' replied Surrain. 'Ooh I'd love to tell the mortals and the old crones the truth when we are married. I'd say, "Listen, you morons, Prince Tal is no more a mortal than I. He comes from Drakohsia and belongs to the Tekwah's People of the Draemid Nation... so there!" Can you imagine the look on their faces?'

The Prince shook his head and laughed. 'You've certainly got a wicked streak, Surrain.'

The little fairy giggled. 'I know. It's great isn't it? I'll tell you something else too. I'm happy most of the time, I adore animals, cherish my surroundings... and pleased you can't read my mind!'

'Oh yeah, and why is that, may I ask?'

'Wouldn't you like to know?' Surrain laughed and changed the subject. 'Hey, are you hungry?'

'Mm, I do feel a bit peckish. In a minute or two I'll go into the kitchen and make a snack.'

'Do you want me to ask Wonda to rustle up a nice meal?' asked Surrain.

'No it's OK. Don't forget, with magic dust and a number of spells up my sleeve, I can't go wrong. Have a rest and I'll look in on you later.'

As the Prince left the bedroom, Surrain stretched out and closed her eyes. After a few moments, a strange rumbling sound disturbed her. The bed began to shudder and Surrain slowly opened her eyes. The little fairy was extremely frightened. Surrain tried calling out to Prince Tal for help, but she couldn't speak, nor could she move a muscle. Surrain felt as if a slab of concrete was crushing her body. Suddenly, a smoky image began to emerge from the floor. The dark apparition grew bigger and stronger. In a matter of seconds, the Grim Reaper had materialized sitting astride his horse. The black steed had silver armour covering his head and forelegs. The horse neighed loudly and reared up, kicking his forelegs over Surrain's bed. The little fairy was paralysed. All she could do was glare at the hooded rider, whose bony finger beckoned her.

Then Surrain heard Prince Tal's footsteps approaching. As the bedroom door opened, the great beast leapt over Surrain's bed. The apparition changed form and a black cloudy mass disappeared into the floor.

The Prince was unaware of Surrain's terrifying encounter. He walked into the bedroom and smiled. 'So, you're still awake? Would you like a bite to eat now?'

To Surrain's relief, the force crushing her body had lifted. She replied, 'No thanks, but I'd appreciate a jug of cold water.'

When the Prince returned with the full jug, Surrain drank the contents in no time at all.

'Goodness me, Surrain, where did that go?' laughed the Prince.

'That's what I'd like to know. Tal, when you were in the kitchen, did you hear anything out of the ordinary?'

Prince Tal shook his head. 'No why?'

Surrain sighed and replied, 'Oh it's nothing. I must have been dreaming. I still feel sleepy, so I'm going to have a rest. Why don't you sit in my bedside chair and have a nap too?'

'I think I will.'

Prince Tal closed his eyes, while Surrain snuggled into her pillow. Almost at once, the little fairy drifted through dreams into the Realm of Isk-us-barooska. Kirrey was waiting for her and they embraced. Surrain's eyes were drawn towards a large radiant cloud. As her eyes adjusted to the light, she saw Prince Tal standing amongst three tall luminous beings.

The little fairy was inquisitive and whispered, 'Kirrey, are those radiant beings angels?'

'Yes,' he replied. 'Angels can differ greatly in form.'

A warm glow enveloped Surrain and she nuzzled into Kirrey. A few moments later, Surrain raised her head and gazed into Kirrey's deep blue eyes. Then his expression changed and Surrain panicked. 'Kirrey, why do you have this look of anguish? What troubles you? Kirrey, what's wrong?' she cried.

Kirrey was suddenly gone and Surrain jolted back into her sleeping body.

At that precise moment, two white boxer dogs pounced on Surrain's bed. The little fairy sat upright while the dogs watched her every move. Then Surrain saw movement behind the animals. For a second, Surrain thought she was seeing things, but No, there they were, three ghostly figures. The apparitions hovered outside the large window opposite Surrain's bed, and she began to tremble. She bent her knees, pulling the bed covers up to her chin. This action brought the dogs closer, although they sat quietly with tilted heads, staring at Surrain. The little fairy's body throbbed with fear and a peculiar sensation came over her. She wanted to alert Prince Tal, but something stopped her. Then, as the ghostly figures closed in on her, she recognised them. They were Princess Debs, Prince Daheyl and Prince Deyn.

The two Princes looked solemn and hovered at the base of Surrain's bed, gazing at her.

Prince Deyn slowly shook his head, while Prince Daheyl whispered, 'It's too late... t-o-o l-a-t-e.'

As the Princes drifted into the background, Princess Debs moved forward. She hovered in between her brothers and looked directly at Surrain, uttering, 'The Seer of Truth...Jozeffri...Seek Jozeffr-i-i-i.'

The Visionary

Surrain was in a dreamy state, nevertheless she heard Princess Debs whisper... 'The Seer of Truth...Jozeffri...Seek Jozeffr-i-i-i.' Those words rang in the little fairy's ears. 'This isn't a riddle,' she said to herself. 'It must be a warning.'

Just then, Prince Daheyl distracted Surrain when he called out to his pets, 'Sasha, Nelson... heel.'

Without any hesitation, the dogs scampered off the bed in mid-air, and headed towards their master. Then all the apparitions began to drift away.

Surrain nudged Prince Tal. He woke with a start and sat upright gasping. 'Surrain, did you see those ghostly figures disappearing through the window?'

Surrain was surprisingly calm. She sighed and replied, 'Yes I did. They are the past rulers of this kingdom, but something is not right. I had to wake you because I wasn't sure if I was dreaming. I needed both of us to see the same thing.'

Even though Prince Tal was taken by surprise, his reply gave Surrain peace of mind. 'I can assure you... that was no dream. I saw five apparitions and they vanished into thin air.'

All of a sudden Surrain's health took a turn for the worse. She grasped her stomach and groaned in pain.

Prince Tal was distressed by Surrain's setback and began to panic. 'Surrain you've gone deathly pale. Is there anything I can do?'

'Could you get my wand? She's in the kitchen.'

'Of course... I won't be a sec.'

The Prince moved hastily and returned with Wonda. 'I do hope Vienne eradicated all the poison when she revived you.'

'Mm,' muttered Surrain, knowing quite well her recovery wasn't due to Vienne. Then the pain increased and Surrain groaned again. The little fairy doubled over. She was in agony and buried her head in her pillow. As Surrain began to rock to and fro, she cried out, 'Something awful is happening to me. This pain is unbearable and it's travelled across my back. Ooh... now I know what Princess Debs meant.'

'Surrain, you're trembling and your face is grey. What more can I do?'

Surrain's breathing became erratic and she broke out in a cold sweat. The little fairy ran a flannel across her face and glanced at Prince Tal, 'Water... Please get me some more cold water.'

Once again the Prince returned with a jug of water and Surrain drank the contents.

Prince Tal sighed as he tried to make light of the situation. 'I'd really like to know where all that liquid's going.'

'Me too,' replied Surrain. 'No matter how much water I drink, I still feel hot and thirsty.'

Surrain placed the wand in the centre of her bed and whispered, 'Wonda, Wonda.'

A tiny head popped out of the slender rod. Wonda took one look at Surrain and knew she was in grave danger. 'Tell me quickly, Surrain, how can I be of assistance?'

'Please invoke the Visionary, Jozeffri.'

'Consider it done,' said Wonda.

Prince Tal sat on the edge of Surrain's bed and they both watched Wonda perform her task.

The tiny wand rose to a vertical position and spun round three times. A look of surprise appeared on Wonda's face and she threw her arms open, 'Surrain, the visionary was on his way before I called upon him.'

'OK. Thank you, Wonda.'

The wand closed her eyes and disappeared into her rod. Then the Prince took Wonda and placed her on the windowsill in the kitchen. When Prince Tal returned to the bedroom, he closed the door and sat in the chair. He noticed the colour in Surrain's face had turned from ashen to pale green. Then something else caught his eye, a mass of white smoke seeping under the closed door.

The Prince pointed and whispered, 'Surrain, look at that.'

They stared at a misty cloud as it began to take shape.

Within seconds, the rugged grandeur of Wizard Jozeffri had materialized. J. smiled at the couple and glided towards Surrain holding his personal manual, The Book of Shadows. Jozeffri wore a black hooded cloak, showing a little of his spiky fair-hair. He lowered his head and said, 'Greetings.' Then he spoke regarding the matter at hand. 'My dear, you are scourged with blight. And it's too late for an anti-dote. You require my immediate attention, so I will begin at once.'

'Can I assist you in any way?' asked the Prince.

'Here, hold my book,' replied Wizard J. passing his ancient manual across.

'Surrain, this will cause you a great deal of discomfort, but it has to be done. Lie on your stomach with your hands by your side. And be still.'

Wizard Jozeffri turned down the quilt. 'Oh dear...your wings are in a dreadful state.' Jozeffri continued and held his hand just above Surrain's nightdress. He uttered a few magic words and the nightgown slowly parted down the middle, unfolding outwards.

A pulsating mass of green lumps was revealed. Wizard J. applied a little pressure to Surrain's spine and she cried out in pain.

Then Jozeffri stood back and sighed. 'I was unable to attend earlier,' he said. 'I accompanied Grudesso, the winged Gargoyle, to a Witches Assembly. As you know, the gathering is held in the Outer Realm of Menoosa, and Grudesso cannot enter that realm alone... Now then, I know Greega did his best for you, but the anti-dote was far too weak. The substance was devoured by these green devils. They thrive on fluid and have multiplied at an alarming rate due to your massive intake of water. Surrain, some of the eggs have already hatched and the worms are expanding under your flesh. That's why you are in so much pain. What a mess.' He sighed. 'After Vienne uttered her spell, I saw this disturbing event unfold. Nevertheless, I am present now and I will rid you of these torments. So fear not, Surrain.' Wizard J. beckoned the Prince, who was standing near the window. 'Come here, Tal. Turn your sight to this.'

The Prince shook his head. 'No,' he replied. 'I saw Surrain's neck earlier. I'm sorry, but my stomach is weak and cannot cope with such repugnance.'

Jozeffri concealed the pulsating mass by covering Surrain's shoulders with her quilt.

'My dear Fairy Queen, even though you invoked me, I took it upon myself to be present. I heard news of your revival but, as a seer,

I knew something was amiss. I gazed into the water and behold, I knew then my presence would be needed.'

'Thank you J. but please don't joke about me being a Fairy Queen. Even if the title was bestowed upon me I would not accept it.'

Wizard J. changed his tone. 'This is foolish talk. You must and you will.'

Surrain sighed. 'Always the optimist... This poison is destroying my very heart and you're talking as if my future is set out.'

'It is,' he replied. 'You of all fairies should know that. Your future has been foretold and I am here to put things right. Surrain let me explain something quickly. For a few seconds you did pass over. You crossed the fine line between life and death. You see, once this green croag beetle has got a hold, its host dies shortly after. But it wasn't your time, so the insect inside you became dormant. I know Kirrey helped you to regain consciousness... hence your awakening. However, due to Vienne's intervention a little earlier, the beetle woke up with a vengeance. The green croag changed its habit and is reproducing on a massive scale. To be honest, Surrain, if I wasn't here to eradicate the creature, I'm afraid the young of these invertebrates would eat you away in a matter of days. Right, before I create a suitable atmosphere, a little preparation is needed. First of all the bed needs to be moved. Then I'll cast a large circle.'

'J. what should I do?' asked the Prince.

'Do nothing. Just stay within the circle at all times.'

The Wizard mumbled a little magic and the bed slid to the centre of the room. Jozeffri continued. With the palm of his left hand facing the wooden floor, he walked clockwise round the bed and created an invisible circle. When the edges of the imaginary circle touched, twelve white esoteric symbols appeared making the circle clearly visible. Then J. grabbed a handful of salt from his right hand pocket. He sprinkled the granular substance over the symbols, thus preventing other entities from entering the circle.

Although Surrain was in pain, her inquisitive nature got the better of her. 'Vienne didn't do any of these preparations. Are they necessary?'

Jozeffri sighed and replied, 'Oh yes. And don't start me off about Vienne! I can assure you, there is method in my madness. Now be still, Surrain.'

Wizard J. turned down the duvet once again, revealing the small pulsating lumps.

Prince Tal showed some interest in Wizard Jozeffri's work and said, 'Well I've certainly learned a thing or two today.'

Jozeffri laughed aloud. 'You've seen nothing yet,' he replied dusting the salt from his hand. 'Stay where you are and keep a watchful eye, you'll learn a lot more... The Book,' requested J.

A Genius at Work

Wizard Jozeffri opened the Book of Shadows and laid it in mid-air. Then he lifted his arm up towards the windows. With a flick of the wrist, the curtains swished together. 'It's time for some light,' he said.

> 'GLOWING ORBS ILLUMINATE THIS ROOM,
> LET BRIGHTNESS SHINE, RESEMBLE FULL MOONS.'

Five small balls of light appeared and hovered around the ceiling. A moment later J. turned to his precious book. He wafted his hand across the manual, flicking the pages over. Then the appropriate spell appeared. Jozeffri glanced at the wording, closed the book, and uttered the magic formula.

Without any warning, a thunderous blast shook the cottage. Seconds later, a bolt of lightning ripped through Surrain's bedroom. The electrical force produced a blue zigzag effect, emitting flashes and sparks. The tiny orbs were terrified and squeaked with fear as they darted about, trying to find a place of safety. After a little while, calm and quietness filled the room.

A bronze dagger (athame) lay across Jozeffri's open hands. Wizard J. didn't waste any time. He raised his magical knife and began to chant.

> 'OH DIVINE ONE, CREATOR OF ALL,
> HEAR MY PLEA, THIS URGENT CALL.
> DO WHAT THY WILL, WITH POWER UNTOLD
> UNTO MY HANDS, FIERY FLAMES UNFOLD.'

The athame began to glow with intense heat. Then Jozeffri held the red-hot dagger over Surrain's back. With slow motions, he moved the wide blade across her flesh. When that task was completed he laid the athame in mid-air beside his Book of Shadows. Jozeffri glanced down at his hands and they ignited. Within seconds they were ablaze and Wizard J. returned to the little fairy's bedside.

'Surrain, I am going to pass my hands across your back and over your shoulders. As I destroy these green demons, you will most definitely feel a burning sensation. Close your eyes go with it, and then my Fairy Queen, all will be well.'

Wizard J. turned round and once again he wafted his hand over the pages of his manual. The book opened at the appropriate spell, then closed.

For a second, Prince Tal thought he saw a hooded monk holding Wizard J.'s ancient book and athame. The Prince closed his eyes and looked again. There was nothing there, just the book and dagger in mid-air. Prince Tal glanced at Jozeffri and whispered, 'Did I just see a monk by any chance?'

'You did indeed. He is my guide,' replied J. 'Now I must get on.' Jozeffri held his burning palms over the nape of Surrain's neck; then proceeded to move his hands across and down the small of her back, chanting the following verse three times...

'OH SPIRIT OF FIRE, I CALL UPON THEE,
FLAME OF DESTRUCTION, THOU WILT BE.
INTO MY HANDS I COMMAND THY POWER,
BURN OUT THESE DEVILS WITHIN THE HOUR.'

Surrain gritted her teeth and tears rolled down her cheeks. As the pain intensified, the little fairy lost consciousness.

Meanwhile, Jozeffri's closed book began to emit eerie groans. The Ancient Manuscript opened wide and grey mist began to rise from its centre. The hazy substance rose up a little and oozed down towards the floor. Within seconds, five Shadow Monks materialized. These ghost-like spectres wore dark hooded cassocks and stood on the inside of the circle. They were linked by a glowing ring of electrical energy, which penetrated each of them at waist height. As they stood with folded arms, they began to hum in a deep repetitive way.

Prince Tal had never experienced anything like this before. He didn't want to make any noticeable movements, so he shuffled towards the end of Surrain's bed, resting his hands on the wrought iron base.

Wizard J. had completed the three verses and silence descended. After a short time, dull rhythmic hums filled the room again. The five monks standing with lowered heads began to fade and change form. A smoky mass appeared. It whirled round the circle and up towards the ceiling. The droning hums dwindled and the grey mass hovered above Surrain. Without any warning, the rotating mass dropped down and disappeared into Surrain's back.

Jozeffri looked at Prince Tal and said, 'Stay still. Stay calm. This is far from over. Shortly I will begin to chant again.'

During this time, Surrain drifted through dreams into the Realm of Isk-us-barooska. In the dim light she found herself being drawn towards a black arched door. The door opened and no matter how hard she tried, Surrain could not escape from the force pulling her inside. All of a sudden the door slammed shut and Surrain stood alone. The large room, lit by an unknown source, was shrouded in light mist. Sorrowful cries, weeping and murmurs encircled the little fairy.

Surrain felt anxious and frightened. She widened her eyes and looked round fearfully. 'Who's there?' she cried. Surrain questioned herself. 'What am I doing here? Where is this unfamiliar place?'

Through the clouds of mist, pale-faced men, women and children drifted closer to Surrain. These ghostly beings approached from every angle. They held out their arms and cried for help in a pitiful manner. Surrain felt trapped. There was nowhere to turn, no place to hide. Tears streamed down Surrain's face and, in a panic, she cried out for her angel. 'KIRREY...! KIRREY, where are you?'

Within an instant Kirrey appeared before her eyes. Surrain grabbed his gown. She pulled Kirrey closer and snuggled into him. 'Kirrey, where am I? Who are these poor souls crying out before me? Why didn't I enter the Realm of Isk-us-barooska?'

The voices suddenly stopped and the people vanished, leaving Surrain and Kirrey alone.

The tall dark angel wrapped his flowing robe around the little fairy and whispered, 'Surrain, this IS Isk-us-barooska. You are experiencing severe pain and discomfort, so you were guided in another direction. This location is where the infirm and dead gather.

Look through the veil of mist. Your body is lying still. Can you hear Wizard J. chanting?'

'Yes,' replied Surrain.

'With help, Jozeffri will summon the poisonous beetle out of your system. Listen...'

'I SUMMON YE FLAMES, DESTROYUS THOU WILL,
I COMMAND YE DESTROYUS, POWER TO FULFIL.
EXTORTUS, SPIRALIS, COME UNTO ME,
FLAMMA DESTROYUS, THOU WILT BE...'

'Surrain, watch closely,' said Kirrey.

A stream of grey mist began to rise out from Surrain's back. The hazy substance floated round the edges of the circle and once again the ghostly mist manifested into five Shadow Monks. The hooded entities stood with lowered heads and folded arms. When the ghostly apparitions began to hum, the pages of Wizard Jozeffri's ancient book flicked open. The Shadow Monks suddenly fell to the floor into a dark misty heap. Almost at once, the cloudy phantoms fused together and whirled round the circle. Then the compacted mass rose up and disappeared into the Book of Shadows.

Kirrey sighed. 'Almost over, Surrain... Jozeffri is destroying the insect, its young and the eggs.' The creatures emerged from Surrain's back and spiralled like twisted green worms, ascending into the fiery palms of Wizard Jozeffri. 'My dear Surrain...'tis why such anguish was upon my face... When we stood together, I could sense the beetle about your being. 'Twas no longer dormant and I knew you would have to endure much misery. Thankfully, my despair has lifted. The Great Seer along with Shadow Monks did away with its presence, and their good deed is nearly at an end.'

Surrain gazed into Kirrey's eyes. 'Kirrey, when I am here with you, I exist as a trouble-free spirit. I am at peace. There is no pain or distress. Happiness is plentiful and I want this feeling to go on and on.'

Kirrey smiled and cupped Surrain's face in his hands. 'Surrain, I see much love in your eyes and when you wake-up, you will not lose this feeling. Love will be all around you and your future will be filled with joy. When you open your eyes, you will realise there is much to look forward too. Remember, if ever you need me, I am never too far away.'

'Kirrey, how could I forget? And I've yet to turn to the last page in my book of poems.'

Kirrey kissed Surrain on her forehead. Then as they gazed into each other's eyes, the pair began to drift apart. Kirrey vanished and Surrain gradually became aware of her surroundings. The little fairy relaxed as she heard Wizard Jozeffri recite the following words...

'FLAMMA OF POWER, EXTINGUERE BE GONE!
I THANK YE FOR ATTENDERE... ALL IS DONE.'

The flames covering Jozeffri's palms extinguished. Then the Wizard held his right palm down and walked anti-clockwise round the circle. As J. uttered his magic, the grains of salt were drawn up, disappearing into the palm of his hand. The esoteric symbols gradually faded and vanished without a trace. The Wizard sighed. He took hold of his magical dagger with both hands and held it above his head. This time he recited the following words, closing the ritual...

'OH DIVINE ONE, CREATOR OF ALL,
THANK YOU FOR GUIDANCE, FOR HEARING MY CALL.
OH SPIRITUS PROTECTI, IN DARKNESS AND LIGHT
YE POWER AND FIRE...I CLOSE THIS RITE.'

The Wizard breathed deeply. He placed the athame in mid-air, beside his Book of Shadows. A moment later he moved his hands across the two items and they vanished. Then when he pointed to the curtains, they drew back with a swish.

Prince Tal continued to stand at the base of Surrain's bed and watch in silence.

'My work is nearing completion,' said Jozeffri. 'It's just the healing process now.'

At that very moment, Veela pawed at the bedroom door. 'Can we come in and see Surrain?'

Prince Tal opened the door. Veela and Sovran took one look at the little fairy and scampered under the bed.

Then, squeaks and squeals were heard. It was the orbs, flitting to and fro crying out for help. The tiny creatures could barely be seen due to the bright sunlight beaming through the window. The orbs felt forgotten, so they turned red, yellow, blue and green, seeking attention.

'I've not lost sight of you,' cried Jozeffri, glancing at the darting spheres. The Wizard pointed to each orb in turn and they vanished, leaving behind a multitude of coloured stars.

Wizard J. turned towards Surrain and continued with his magic. He rubbed his hands together and blew into them. With both palms face down, Jozeffri moved his hands across the little fairy's back, healing the wounds. He held his left hand above the nape of Surrain's neck, and her nightdress joined together, becoming intact once again.

Jozeffri sighed and said, 'All done, my dear. You can sit up now. It won't be long before your health is restored.'

Surrain turned over and sat up. Her face looked somewhat peculiar as she held her gurgling stomach.

Prince Tal was puzzled and perched on the edge of the little fairy's bed. He didn't know what to think of her appearance and frowned. 'How do you feel Surrain?'

The little fairy didn't reply. Her face began to change colour, turning every shade of green.

Wizard Jozeffri backed off. He stood opposite Surrain's bed near the window. 'Wait for it, Tal. When Surrain jerks forward, move out of the way...fast!'

Surrain's stomach carried on making strange noises. She began to heave up. Surrain's cheeks bulged and she covered her mouth with her hand. The little fairy leaned over the right side of her bed, where she saw Veela and Sovran. The two wolves, wide-eyed and trembling, stared back at her.

Suddenly, scuttling was heard coming from under the bed and Sovran yelled, 'Let me out of here!'

Jozeffri clicked his fingers, opening the door, and Sovran pelted through it.

By this time Surrain was sitting up, but she couldn't keep the fluid down any longer. The little fairy leant forward and threw up. A green stream of vomit jetted up and out, like a volcanic eruption.

Wizard J. was ready, he pointed to a gaping hole near his feet where the green vomit disappeared, before it touched the floor. Jozeffri knew what to expect, unlike Prince Tal who fell back flabbergasted into Surrain's bedside chair.

Wizard J. nodded and said, 'That's good Surrain. The last of the poison has been expelled from your system.' Jozeffri glanced at the Prince and chuckled. 'Now you can ask Surrain how she feels.'

Veela, as calm as ever, crept from underneath the bed. The grey she-wolf smiled at Surrain and in her soft voice she said, 'We've really missed you, Surrain. Thanks to Wizard Jozeffri, you are back with us.' Moments later, Veela looked at Prince Tal and slowly shook her head. 'I don't know. Typical male, can't cope with anything untoward.'

The Prince jumped out of his seat and yelled, 'When I want your opinion I'll ask for it. Now go outside with Sovran!'

Veela ignored Prince Tal's order. She walked out of the room in her own time and Jozeffri closed the door behind her.

Prince Tal's tone changed and he sat gazing at Surrain. 'You look almost radiant.'

'Only almost,' laughed Surrain. 'I feel great. Cleansed and free. Thank you so much, J.'

'You're welcome, my dear. Now rest. You're still weak and need to regain your strength. I'll move your bed back to its rightful place and leave you in the capable hands of Tal.'

The Wizard pointed to the bed, which returned to its position. Then he stood with folded arms and looked straight at Surrain. He could see that the little fairy was eager to ask a question. 'Before you say a word Surrain, I will put your mind at ease. As it happens, I did see the recent event that took place between you and the old crones. I must say, I was highly amused by the way you handled the situation. Ibsis and Igfreid are not a problem. They only send forth 'mindless threats' as you stated, but if you so wish, I can render them totally powerless.'

Surrain shook her head and replied, 'No, that won't be necessary.'

Jozeffri continued. 'Surrain, the old crones resent you in every sense of the word. Ibsis and Igfreid have dreams that will never be fulfilled. They would like nothing more than to see you perish. You on the other hand are going to experience more than you could ever imagine. Be sure of this, you will visit the Realm of Elfina in Zenith. As you already know, Elfina is filled with the chosen few, who await your arrival. You will surely find Elfina to be the most enchanting place you have ever visited. You will want to stay there, but fear not, you will have a strong reason for not doing so.'

The Prince and Surrain sat together. They listened with interest to Jozeffri, although Surrain was intrigued by his last remark.

Surrain smiled at the Wizard and said, 'Please enlighten me. Tell me the reason why I will not want to stay in such a delightful place.'

Wizard J. slowly shook his head. 'No,' he replied. 'Wait and see. That way you'll have something more to look forward too.'

Surrain knew Jozeffri wouldn't give in and she expressed an element of disappointment.

Nevertheless, Wizard J. handled the little fairy's changing mood in his own way. 'Surrain, straighten that face. You'll be in the Realm of Elfina soon enough,' he said, clasping his hands. 'I know you are seeking information about your time in the woods. So, before I depart, I will quickly explain. My dear, each time your eyes were set upon Princess Debs, Prince Daheyl and Prince Deyn, you were in a dreamy state. In the Realm of Elfina, these three special beings were approached by Yaarg, Prince of Bard. Yaarg is an influential figure in Elfina, and quite unlike any other dweller. Due to his difference, Yaarg is able to erm...to time travel if you will, and choose any age he wishes to be. And, as well as having art and poetry up his sleeve, in Elfina, this well-known personality is Keeper of the Mirror. Yaarg allowed Princess Debs and her two brothers to travel through this vessel, to advise you. 'Twas the only way in which they could communicate. The only aim of Princess Debs, Prince Daheyl and Prince Deyn, was to inform you of impending danger, warning you not to drink any liquid. You did not take heed of this warning Surrain, thus feeding the green croag beetle. Due to your high intake of liquid, you became host to the insect, and it was too late for an anti-dote. The ghostly apparitions failed. The last option was to guide you to summon help.'

Surrain still felt woozy. She sighed and said, 'I wondered why Princess Debs, Prince Daheyl and Prince Deyn were saying it's too late.'

'Well, there you are.'

'Who is Yaarg? And why is he different?' asked Surrain.

Wizard J. sighed and replied, 'I feel that's quite enough for today.' Jozeffri bowed his head to Prince Tal and Surrain. 'I bid you both farewell and look forward to seeing you at the forthcoming event.'

Wizard J.'s exit was just as fascinating as his entrance. Jozeffri lifted his arm, sweeping his cloak around his person. He then turned as if on an axis. As he spun round, he began to shrink. Within seconds he was gone.

Angels, Ghosts and Ghouls

After Wizard J.'s departure, Surrain seemed quite cheerful. She glanced at the Prince and said, 'Tal thanks for being here with me.'

Prince Tal replied, 'I wouldn't have it any other way. Now, is there anything you'd like before I settle down?'

'No, thank you. I just want to have a good sleep.'

'That's fine. I'll leave you to it and I'll get my head down on the sofa.'

The Prince tucked the duvet round Surrain and, as she snuggled into it, he quietly left the room. He made his way to the front door and called out to the wolves, 'Veela, Sovran, do you want to come inside and settle down with me?'

The wolves ambled towards Prince Tal and Sovran just mumbled, 'Yes, we'd appreciate that.'

Prince Tal lay on the sofa, while Veela and Sovran curled up on the fireside rug. Shortly after, the Prince fell into a deep sleep.

Meanwhile, a strange unnerving atmosphere began to unfold in Surrain's bedroom. Although the little fairy felt extremely tired and weak, she woke up to an unsettling feeling of dread and fear. There was nothing in sight. Nevertheless, as Surrain glanced round, her throbbing heart pounded through her weak and frail body and she was filled with apprehension.

All of a sudden the Crimson Cut-throat materialized beside her bed. Surrain was about to call out to Prince Tal, but the evil ghoul held her down and covered her mouth with his bony hand. The hooded entity wrapped his other emaciated hand round Surrain's hair and yanked her head back, baring her neck. Then Surrain saw the ghoul's cut-throat razor. His head burst into flames and the little fairy gazed in horror at the petrified faces of his screaming victims. 'At last,' he sneered

Prince Tal was alerted by Veela and Sovran. The growling wolves dashed to Surrain's room, snarling viciously and clawing at the closed door. As the Prince came round, he heard a frenzied attack taking place. He jumped up and rushed to Surrain's bedroom. Prince

Tal flung the door open, to a silent blood-splattered room. Looking towards the far side of the bed he saw a bedraggled wolf, dripping with blood. The wolf, unsteady on her back legs, let out a long doleful cry. Then she glanced at the gazing trio and collapsed.

Prince Tal made a dash towards the animal, but found instead Surrain, sprawled out in her blood-covered nightdress, lying in a pool of blood. The Prince knelt down and checked her pulse. Seconds later, with his palm down, the Prince began to heal Surrain's deep cuts and torn wings. Then, as he mumbled, the blood staining Surrain's nightdress vanished. He carefully picked up the little fairy's limp body and placed her on the bed. He reached down for the crumpled duvet, which was strewn across the floor, and shook it. To his surprise, a cut-throat razor slid across the wooden floor. 'Now I understand,' he said.

'Poor Surrain... At least she had the power to change form,' cried Sovran.

Veela sighed. 'You're right Sovran. Thankfully Surrain's inner self has saved her. Just imagine how she must have felt, staring into the face of death.'

Meanwhile, Prince Tal covered up the sleeping fairy. He took hold of the razor and pocketed the blade, before proceeding to clean the room. As he moved his open hand across the floor, the blood began to vanish. Veela and Sovran walked towards the bed and curled up near Surrain, while the Prince sat on the edge of her bed.

Prince Tal looked at Veela and Sovran. 'I won't be leaving Surrain alone again, that's for sure.'

Sovran glanced at Prince Tal and said, 'You look tired. Have a rest in Surrain's bedside chair and we'll keep watch.'

'I'll take you up on that,' replied the Prince, and he made himself comfortable.

After a couple of hours, Surrain opened her eyes. The little fairy sat up and glanced at Veela and Sovran, 'I feel quite refreshed. Aw, look at Tal... he's well away.'

Veela and Sovran raised their eyebrows.

'Are you sure you feel OK?' asked Veela.

'Yes, why shouldn't I? Jozeffri did a good job ridding me of that poison.'

Just then Prince Tal stirred. He opened his eyes to find the little fairy bright and cheerful. 'Surrain, are you all right?'

'Of course I am. I was just telling Veela and Sovran that Jozeffri did a marvellous job.'

'No, Surrain. I mean, are you all right after that frenzied attack?'

Surrain thought for a second and replied with a frown, 'Sorry? I don't know what you're talking about.'

Prince Tal was quick to reply. 'It's OK. Just forget it.'

Surrain totally changed the subject. 'Tal, could you bring me my book of poetry. It's in the other room.'

The Prince smiled. 'Certainly,' and he promptly rose to his feet.

After picking up the book, Prince Tal returned to Surrain's bedroom and sat in the bedside chair.

Surrain turned to the last page, to see what Kirrey had written. The little fairy expected to find a message, and to her surprise it was a poetical verse. Surrain ran her eyes over the poem. Then she patted the bedcover. 'Tal, sit here, I want to read you this verse.' The Prince sat on the edge of the bed and Surrain began.

'Peace and Happiness

In Heaven above, look up and see,
Feel everything you mean to me.
I'm in the wind... I'm in the trees,
Blowing around you, that gentle breeze...
I'll always be with you, can't you see?
We cannot part... together our hearts,
Forever meant to be.'

The Prince was clearly riled and muttered, 'Mm...'

Surrain was unaware of Prince Tal's feelings. The little fairy closed her book and held it near to her heart. She smiled and turned to the Prince. 'Ooh, what a touching verse. What do you think about that?'

Prince Tal returned to the bedside chair and replied, 'I wouldn't say that verse is touching? Huh, more like strange.'

Surrain didn't expect such a negative response and she stared at the Prince.

Prince Tal sighed. 'What's the matter? Do you want me to say something I don't mean?'

'No. But that poem is special to me. It's from Kirrey, my Guardian Angel. You could have been a bit more positive.'

'I know who it's from Surrain. I'm sorry... your kind of poetry doesn't interest me. I'm not Yaarg, the Prince of Bard, you know.'

Surrain was roused by that last remark. 'The Prince of Bard...?'

Prince Tal sighed again and in a witty manner he replied, 'Yes... the wondering poet.'

Although Surrain began to feel tired, she was curious and asked the Prince another question. 'Do you know much about Yaarg?'

'Enough,' he said.

'Don't stop there. What does Yaarg look like? I'm sure I've met him.'

'Surrain, if you'd met him you'd know. He's a memorable character...tall, slim and pale...very pale. Well he would be, wouldn't he? Yaarg usually wears a wide-brimmed hat covering his fair-hair and a long coat.' Prince Tal frowned. 'Sometime ago, I saw Yaarg, and on that occasion he looked very different. He appeared to be quite youthful. He was in Magentis Castle, playing a game of chess with the Crimson Cut-throat, and I disturbed them.'

Surrain was intrigued. 'That's amazing. Why didn't you tell me?'

The Prince raised his eyebrows and replied, 'Why should I? Besides, there was nothing to tell. But this will interest you. When I met Yaarg in the Realm of Elfina in Zenith, he was much older. Yaarg has visited Magentis Castle on a number of occasions and always appears middle-aged. As Wizard Jozeffri said earlier...in Elfina, Yaarg is the Keeper of the Mirror. If Yaarg decides to leave Elfina to visit the past or present, he goes through certain motions. First of all he chooses his destination, and the age he wishes to be; then he moves his hand across the face of the mirror in a certain way...like a control if you will, and he enters the mirror. When you meet Yaarg, ask him about his travels and how he gets there. But I must warn you. Yaarg talks in riddles... he's quite a romancer and can talk a glass-eye to sleep.'

In her tiredness, Surrain daydreamed throughout Prince Tal's explanation. Elfina in Zenith fascinated Surrain and her wandering mind began to romanticize about this wondrous land. When Prince

Tal finished explaining, the little fairy cried out, 'When did you visit the Realm of Elfina in Zenith?'

'Sometime ago... That's another story for another day. And before I forget, Surrain, make of it what you will, but angels are neither male nor female.'

Surrain shook her head and said, 'Well Kirrey is a male.'

The Prince sighed. 'I'm sure we've had this conversation before, Surrain. I told you, Kirrey is a spiritual being...a pure source of light. There is no he or she, so don't be telling me otherwise.'

Surrain sighed deeply. A moment later she said, 'Last time I entered Isk-us-barooska, I saw you standing in the centre of three angelic beings. Those angels were very different to Kirrey. They were much taller, with quivering wings...like bees. Oh, and one angel had two wings, one had three and the other had four pairs of featherless wings.'

The Prince smiled, 'Mm... and were the angels male or female?' he asked.

Surrain was becoming increasingly irritated by Prince Tal. She sighed and replied, 'I don't know! Their faces were obscure, due to the radiance surrounding them.'

Prince Tal saw a situation arising, so he said, 'Calm down. I thought we were having a conversation here. Listen Surrain, there's a lot to learn about angels, and I know very little. So before you go off on one again, let me explain and I'll tell you what I do know. There are many angels...billions in fact...only the Divine knows their true number. Angels are winged messengers, created from the highest form of spiritual light. There are angels who arrange all matters accordingly and each angel knows its place. There are angels of mercy, angels of punishment... soldiers to soul takers. As you know, the chief soul taker is the angel of death. This angel is assigned to taking lives, and has many helpers. There are also nineteen angels who guard the seven gates of hell. They are huge creatures, way beyond our comprehension. On a lighter note, two angels are appointed to each and every one of us. One angel sits on our right shoulder and records our good deeds, while the other angel sits on our left shoulder, and records our bad deeds.' All of a sudden Prince Tal laughed aloud, 'Surrain! I knew there was an air of familiarity about you. I've just remembered the place where I saw you for the very first time. It was in my dreams.'

Surrain giggled. 'Oh yeah, and you expect me to believe that?'

'It's true. Honestly!'

Prince Tal and Surrain continued to chat, whiling away the time. Before they knew it, darkness had descended on the fairy kingdom and the weary couple fell fast asleep.

The Ancient Script
And a Visitant

The beginning of a new day was dawning. Prince Tal and Surrain woke up to the sweet sound of fairy blue birds chirping on the windowsill. The Prince yawned and stretched his arms in the air. He was aching due to sleeping in the chair, unlike Surrain, who'd had a wonderful sleep.

Prince Tal walked towards the bathroom and said, 'I'm just having a hot shower to ease my aching bones.'

Meanwhile, Veela and Sovran were comforted by Surrain's recovery. The two wolves stood up and shook their furry bodies. They glanced at the little fairy and a look of satisfaction swept across their faces.

Surrain jumped out of bed. She opened the front door and cried out, 'What a beautiful sunny morning! Veela, Sovran, come on...have a wander about.'

Just then, Prince Tal left the bathroom looking bright and cheerful. 'All yours Surrain...'

'Thanks, Tal. I'm going to pamper myself and have a relaxing bath. I won't be long.'

The Prince smiled and on his way to the living room he caught sight of a scroll lying on the table. He picked up the parchment and sat on the sofa, muttering, 'Now what have we here?' He unrolled the scroll and quietly read the first line of the ancient script. Suddenly, a radiant light shone out from the paper, dazzling the Prince. The light quickly faded and the scroll unravelled by itself staying open on a particular spell. As Prince Tal read the verse, a dark eerie shadow passed over him. The Prince shuddered. He tried to roll up the scroll, but it was impossible. Then he heard sobbing coming from within the parchment. As the Prince's eyes were fixed on the scroll, the Crimson Cut-throat appeared. This evil entity, hovering above wailing souls, waved his razor to and fro. Prince Tal knew what he had to do. He moved his hand across the parchment whilst reciting a prayer. Then, a dark misty apparition rose out of the parchment and into Surrain's mirror. All of a sudden, the scroll rolled up and soared into the air, promptly falling onto the floor.

At that very moment, Surrain walked into the room. The little fairy was surprised to see the scroll lying in front of her, so she picked it up and said, 'Tal, what's this doing here?'

'Surrain, you wouldn't believe me if I told you. Who gave you that evil piece of work?'

'The sorceress,' she replied. 'When I visited Vienne, I saw the scroll on her cabinet. As I had a peek, I was fascinated and felt impelled to own the ancient script. To my surprise, Vienne said she didn't want the scroll, so I brought it home with me.'

'Surrain, in the wrong hands, that parchment is deadly. It needs to be destroyed... And I'm not joking.'

The little fairy didn't argue. She gave the scroll to Prince Tal and said, 'I'll take your word for it. Here, get rid of the parchment. I couldn't understand the cryptic writing anyway.'

The Prince sighed, 'Thank goodness for that.' Then he made his way outside. Prince Tal walked behind the cottage and placed the scroll on the ground in front of him. He began to recite another prayer and the scroll unravelled. Weeping and ghostly cries called out for help. Smoke started to rise from the parchment and it suddenly burst into flames. Prince Tal watched as shadows of wailing spirits rose out of the flames. At last the screaming souls were released. The spirits turned and smiled at Prince Tal before being drawn into the forest. And there they were laid to rest beneath the Sacred Oak...all but one.

The ritual frightened Veela and Sovran, so much, they ran for safety into the cottage.

Meanwhile, the Crimson Cut-throat glided towards Prince Tal and stood directly behind him. The Prince had a good intuition and felt the presence of an evil entity. He quickly turned round and came face to face with the red-hooded ghoul. A strong whistling wind suddenly blew back the Crimson Cut-throat's hood, revealing his skull. The spirit roared and Prince Tal saw more pitiful faces amongst the flames, deep inside the entity's throat.

Prince Tal scowled at the Crimson Cut-throat. He then wafted his hand across his face, trying to get rid of the disgusting odour. 'Listen sewer breath,' he said, 'even though you are the epitome of evil, you don't frighten me. One day your time will come, and like everyone else, you will be judged accordingly.'

The Crimson Cut-throat snarled and laughed hysterically, before vanishing.

Prince Tal smiled and returned to the cottage dusting his hands. 'All done... Thanks for letting me destroy that scroll, Surrain. When I see Vienne, I'll make a point of asking her why she gave you such an evil piece of work.'

Surrain sighed, 'Ooh don't, please. Vienne did say the ancient scroll was used quite often, even during a black mass.'

Prince Tal shook his head. He made his way to the sofa and sat beside Surrain.

The little fairy's emotions were running high and she said, 'I'm glad that scroll is gone. Let's put everything behind us. I feel like I've been given a new lease of life.'

The Prince wrapped his arm round her shoulders and smiled. 'All right Surrain, our future begins today. Now, I've got to think about our wedding and make the appropriate plans. The social gathering is nearly upon us and shortly after that event, we'll have our wedding.'

Surrain snuggled into the Prince and whispered, 'Don't worry. I'm sure everything will fall into place.'

Just as Surrain had finished her sentence, there was a tap on the window. Prince Tal opened the front door. He looked right and left, but couldn't see a soul, so he returned to the sofa.

'There was no-one there,' he sighed. 'It wouldn't surprise me if it was Roster being silly. That owl can be a menace at times.'

Surrain disagreed. 'Roster wouldn't be so inconsiderate. Not after the recent events.'

Unbeknown to Prince Tal and Surrain, a small coil of smoke had followed the Prince back into the room.

Veela and Sovran were uneasy. The wolves stood up and growled, staring at the whirling mist.

Prince Tal glanced at the wolves and sighed, 'What's wrong now?' Then he saw the coil of smoke, drifting towards him.

He reached out to grab it, but Surrain pushed his hand down. 'No, Tal, don't do that,' whispered the little fairy. 'This is intriguing. It could be something weird and wonderful.'

'Or a spine-chilling entity, sinister and disturbing,' added the Prince.

'Ooh, Tal. Let's watch the mist before it vanishes. Veela, Sovran, you hush too.'

The wolves stopped growling and lay beside the fire, staring at their unexpected visitor.

The cloudy particles began to expand, growing taller and wider. Then the smoke materialized into a silver leafless tree. As the branches reached the ceiling, green leaves sprouted out, covering the tree.

The little fairy noticed three glowing baubles hanging amongst the branches. She smiled and said to the Prince, 'Relax. Don't perch on the end of your seat. Sit back and enjoy the show.'

Prince Tal sighed and said, 'After the recent events, I'm wondering what else to expect.'

All of a sudden, there was a loud scraping noise, as the tree began to sink into the wooden floor. Prince Tal, Surrain and the two wolves were mesmerised. A cloud of dust was left behind and before the particles had a chance to settle, Casey appeared. The young wizard, wearing a black hooded cloak, held the three baubles in his hands, and he began to juggle the trinkets. Casey dropped the ornaments and chuckled to himself. The glowing balls burst open and Casey's three cats emerged from them.

Surrain applauded. 'Very good Casey... That was brilliant. You've improved immensely.'

'Thank you, Surrain, but I haven't finished yet. I know you like trees, so I'm congratulating you with an early wedding gift.' Casey blew across the palm of his hand. Suddenly, a white envelope and a tiny fir tree appeared on the little fairy's lap.

Prince Tal was silent and calm, waiting in anticipation, for Casey's next move...

Meanwhile, Surrain sat back and smiled at the odd gift. 'Thank you.'

'You're welcome,' said Casey. Then he continued. 'The letter is from my dad and the tree is a special gift from me. In the outside world, huge trees, including pine trees, are cut down for their commercial value. And listen to this, each year during mid-winter, there is a certain festival, and pagan mortals buy a pine tree for their home. It sounds silly, but the mortals decorate the branches with trinkets, buy presents for each other, and pile them beneath the tree.'

Surrain smiled at Casey and said, 'Thank you for your gift and for enlightening us.'

Without saying another word, the youngster clicked his fingers and his cats jumped into his pocket. Seconds later, the young wizard spun round and vanished in a puff of smoke.

'Well well,' said Surrain. 'Casey's magical skills have improved no-end. And look at this miniature fir tree. It's so cute. What a thoughtful gift.'

Surrain began to twiddle the tiny cones covering the tree. Without any warning, a stern, bearded face appeared in the centre of the branches. The conifer cried out, 'And who might you be?'

Surrain was so shocked when the tree spoke that she sprang out of her seat, throwing the fir tree in the air. Prince Tal acted instinctively and caught the evergreen, before it crashed to the floor.

The little fairy was trembling. 'Casey didn't say it was a talking tree. And it has a funny accent.'

Prince Tal shook his head and laughed. 'You should have seen your face, Surrain. It was a picture.' As the Prince looked closely at the miniature conifer, he noticed it was frowning.

Then the tree yelled, 'I do not have a funny accent.'

Prince Tal chuckled and replied, 'Quite right. You're from Scotland, a wonderful place in the outside world. Here, Surrain, take the prickly so and so and talk to it yourself.'

Surrain sat on the sofa and held the conifer in her cupped hands. She gazed at the tree, with its tiny ageing face, long loose greying hair and goatee beard. 'So, you're from Scotland?' asked the little fairy.

'Aye... and what of it...? I'm proud to say I'm a Scot through and through.'

Surrain wasn't impressed and spoke her mind. 'You are very loud and aggressive for such a tiny specimen.'

The tree's expression changed. He scowled at Surrain and replied abruptly, 'Loud, eh? Huh, not as loud as I used to be. And who are you to call me wee?'

'I'm Surrain, Faerie of the Forest.'

• 'Huh, never heard of you. My name is Treeb the Leanin' Fir.' Then he sighed. 'Ooh the forest... the forest.' Treeb's pine needles changed from green to red and he yelled, 'No-one gave you permission to play with my cones...so back off!'

Surrain knew Treeb was annoyed, so she apologised. 'I'm sorry, it won't happen again.'

'Damn right it won't! Now, Missy, what am I doing here with you?'

'Well... trees are very special to me, so, you're a wedding gift from Casey the young wizard.'

The tiny conifer lowered his tone. 'Oh aye... Casey, the wee bairn who saved me life... What a day that was. The mortals were in the forest, chopping down every tree they came across. I was about to be axed, when Casey materialized beside me. The youngster certainly gave those mortals a deserving fright. They're evil people. They don't give a thought to the countless creatures whose homes they are destroying. They're crushing the very heart of the ecosystem and that's criminal. Man's greed is incomprehensible. Why don't they understand that every living creature has feelings? I'm talking about mammals, birds, insects, reptiles, sea-life and the abundance of creatures yet to be discovered. Ooh...' he sighed. 'Let's get back to why I'm here, before I shed my needles with rage and sadness. Casey pointed his finger at a few of us trees and darkness enveloped us. We woke up to find ourselves in another world. And, to top it all, we were miniature versions of our former selves. I'm glad Casey saved us, but I'm not sure about being so small.'

Surrain tried to reassure Treeb and said, 'You'll soon adapt.'

But the tiny tree wasn't having any of it. 'Adapt? What if I don't want to adapt? Oh, put me down.'

Surrain sighed, and she strode over the sleeping wolves, placing Treeb on the mantelpiece.

'What a strange little tree,' said Surrain, as she picked up Jozeffri's letter. 'Let's take a look inside this envelope. Maybe there are more surprises in here.'

Prince Tal sighed deeply and replied, 'I suppose I'll have to get used to this crazy world I'm marrying into. So, what's Jozeffri got to say?'

'Wow. Wizard J.'s been really busy,' she replied. Surrain leapt from her seat and ran to her bedroom. The little fairy returned moments later smiling.

'Dare I ask what that burst of energy was all about?'

Surrain was buzzing with excitement and could barely contain herself. 'Just listen to this. J.'s already seen Grand Master Meidi. Our wedding has been arranged and my beautiful gown is hanging behind my bedroom door. There's also a bundle of gold ceremonial coats, for Jameela and the animals leading the procession. In the centre of each jacket is a black emblem depicting Tekwah's Star. And guess what? The initials of the crest T. and S. are in large black letters on either side of each coat...they look brilliant.'

The Prince smiled and replied, 'The coats sound perfect. So when is the wedding to take place?'

'In four days.'

'Four days?!' he cried out. 'We'd better shake ourselves. You know, in the outside world, that date will be the 8th January.'

'Ooh... I can't wait,' giggled Surrain. Then she continued reading the letter. 'Roster will be flying round the kingdom, informing the residents. All we have to do is visit Meidi for a chat.'

'Surrain, do you feel well enough to visit Meidi now?'

The little fairy replied, 'I feel tired, but it's not as if I'll be doing any strenuous work. I'll give Veela and Sovran a nudge and we'll all go together.'

The moment Surrain rose to her feet, Treeb tried to catch her attention. The tiny tree began to buzz and seconds later his needles flashed in a sequence of bright colours...red, green, orange and blue.

Surrain couldn't help but notice Treeb's flickering lights, so she leant towards him and said, 'Hello Treeb. What's the matter?'

'Hello lass. Sorry for being offensive earlier. Will you accept a sincere apology?'

Surrain replied, 'Of course,' and she moved her face closer to the tiny tree. 'Treeb, you have a sorrowful look on your face. Are you feeling downhearted?'

Treeb lowered his gaze and uttered, 'I'm a wee bit lonely sitting here on my own.'

Surrain smiled. 'Ooh, I've just had a brainwave. Come on, my little fellow. I have the perfect companion for you.' Surrain picked up the pine tree and took him into the kitchen. The little fairy placed Treeb on the windowsill and whispered, 'Wonda, I have a surprise for you.'

Wonda popped her head out of the end of her rod and smiled. 'Hi Surrain, a surprise you say?'

'Yes. Look to your left. I'd like you to meet Treeb.'

Wonda was overjoyed and cried out in her squeaky voice, 'Ooh, my very own friend.'

The tiny wand and miniature fir tree hit it off instantly. Treeb's eyes widened and he had a big smile on his face. 'Hi Wonda, I'm Treeb the Leanin' Fir.'

'Hello,' replied Wonda, rather shyly. 'Ooh, I must say, your accent is new to me...and very nice.'

Treeb looked bashful and flushed with embarrassment. 'Thank you, Wonda,' he mumbled. 'I'm a Scot's pine. Once upon a time, I lived in a beautiful wood in Scotland, a land filled with pine trees just like me.' Treeb suddenly swayed from side to side, and his needles burst into a series of bright colours.

This odd couple were as happy as could be. So Surrain left them to it and joined Prince Tal.

Evil Within

Surrain left Treeb and Wonda nattering on the windowsill and returned to the living room. The little fairy glanced at Prince Tal and said, 'Treeb and Wonda are really chuffed with each other. It's as if they've been reunited.'

The two wolves, curled up by Prince Tal's feet peered at Surrain. But the Prince wasn't impressed. 'Surrain, you've been messing about in the kitchen for ages. Do you want to visit the Grand Master or not?'

'Yes, of course I do.' Then Surrain leant over Veela and Sovran. As she tickled their ears, she said, 'We're off to Magentis Castle. Are you coming along?'

'OK,' said Veela.

Sovran yawned.

'Look lively you two,' cried the Prince. 'We'll go to Magentis Castle the easy way. It'll save time and your energy.'

Veela and Sovran rose to their feet. After they had shaken their furry bodies, Veela said, 'We're ready.'

'Right, so let's go,' replied Surrain.

'Oh no,' cried the Prince. 'I don't believe this! I totally forgot about today's social gathering. It's the yearly get-together for the mortal community. They'll be making their way to Magentis Castle right now.'

Surrain understood and said, 'You go ahead. The visit to Meidi can wait until tomorrow.'

'No, Surrain. We'll go to my chambers and get ready for the occasion. Then we'll call on Meidi, and go to the Great Hall together.'

All of a sudden a look of horror swept across Surrain's pale face. The little fairy felt breathless and fell backwards into her fireside chair.

This was quite unexpected and Prince Tal rushed towards her. 'Surrain, what's the matter?'

After a couple of seconds Surrain breathed deeply and, with the flat of her hand across her chest, she slowly raised her head. Surrain looked alarmed as she glared at Prince Tal, and cried out, 'Have I got to go? You know the mortals hate me.'

'Don't be silly, Surrain. We're a couple and you'll be by my side when our guests arrive.'

'But...But... they'll be a room full of two-faced mortals. Ooh, I don't know if I can cope.'

The Prince sighed, 'Surrain, please. That's nonsense. Don't take any notice of the mortals. Just stay by my side looking pretty. We'll show them. You'll be the Belle of the Ball in your long fancy gown.'

Although Surrain was still agitated, the Prince had talked her round. 'All right, Tal, I'm willing to go along. But if I get distressed in any way, I'm leaving the Great Hall and I'll wait for you in your chambers.'

'That's fine with me. Now come on, Surrain, let's make a move.'

The little fairy uttered a few magic words, but to her dismay, nothing happened.

'Oops,' said Sovran.

Surrain was too weak to carry out a spell successfully and this clearly upset her. 'See...The day's already started to go wrong. I don't know if I can do this.'

The Prince put his arm around Surrain and comforted her. 'This is only a temporary setback. You can't expect to make an overnight recovery. Here, help yourself to a sprinkling of magic dust. You might need it later,' he said, passing Surrain his amulet.

'Thanks, Tal. I'll take enough for a few spells, just in case.' Surrain took a pinch of the powdery substance and stored it in a tiny phial, in the centre of her diamond necklace.

Veela sat beside the little fairy and gazed into her eyes. 'Surrain, see if you can fly...'

'That's a good idea, Veela.' Surrain stood up and fluttered her wings. Then she rose up and flew round the room. 'Wheee...at least I can fly.'

The Prince nodded and said, 'You're getting there slowly but surely. Now don't overdo it, Surrain. Come on.'

Surrain landed gracefully, in between Veela and Sovran.

'Time to go,' said the Prince, and he opened his amulet. He threw a sprinkling of magic dust, whilst uttering a spell. Then they all vanished.

During this time, Nimra and Laegore stood in the courtyard talking. Without any warning, the sound of clattering hooves and carriage wheels cut-short their conversation. The two Dog Men turned their heads, and watched with interest as the first of three horse-drawn coaches made its way over the drawbridge. Suddenly, the small groom (known as a tiger boy) leapt off his tiny seat at the rear of the coach; the groom raced to the front of the grand coach and led the two huge horses across the cobbled courtyard, bringing them to a halt near the stables. When the three coaches were standing side by side, each groom opened the coach door; the high-flying occupants, dressed in their fineries, stepped out of their coach onto the cobbles. Trailing behind were crowds of mortals... these second-class citizens nattered as they trudged up Butterfly Hill.

Then, Prince Tal, Surrain, Veela and Sovran materialized beside Nimra and Laegore, startling the patrolling guards.

Nimra gasped and took a step back. 'Oh, Sir, for a moment there, you gave me a fright.' The Dog Man soon regained composure and greeted the couple. 'Good morning. And I believe Congratulations are in order?'

The little fairy looked at the oncoming crowd, walking over the drawbridge. Surrain seemed uneasy... nevertheless, she smiled and replied, 'That's right and thank you, Nimra.'

Laegore nodded his head. He looked at the couple side on, trying to conceal the left side of his face. Then he said, 'Morning Sir... morning Surrain. I'm pleased to see you're making good progress, Surrain. We've been really worried about you, and I speak for all the Dog Men. I'd also like to express my good wishes to you both.'

Although Surrain was still smiling, she was aware something was wrong. 'Thank you, Laegore,' she replied. Surrain didn't want to question Laegore at this particular time, as the mortals who walked by made her feel edgy, but Prince Tal's face said it all.

While Surrain was chatting, the Prince had been staring at both Dog Men. Prince Tal was alarmed by their appearance. He took a handkerchief out of his pocket and said, 'Here, Nimra, take this hankie, there's blood seeping from your ear. I've noticed your eye is swollen too.' Then the Prince spoke to the other guard. 'Laegore, why are your eyes puffed up? And how did you get that gash down the left side of your cheek? What's going on?'

The two guards lowered their heads, refusing to speak.

Surrain noticed Greega. The Dog Man was standing in the open doorway, leading to the entrance hall and listening to the conversation. As they gazed at each other, Surrain sensed Greega's anguish.

All of a sudden Prince Tal's tone changed. He yelled at Nimra and Laegore, startling Surrain and the passing crowd. 'Out with it men... I demand an answer. You've been fighting, haven't you?'

Nimra and Laegore were shocked by Prince Tal's accusation. The guards instantly raised their heads and together they cried out, 'No, Sir.'

As Nimra dabbed the blood trickling down his neck, he looked at Prince Tal with sorrow in his eyes. The guard was nervous, but he plucked up courage and said, 'Sir, it was Grand Master Meidi who did this to us. I beg you... please don't mention this matter to him.'

The Prince was furious and once again he yelled, 'Why not? Meidi is well out of order. Laegore, what has possessed a person of his status to mistreat you both in this dreadful way?'

Laegore shook his head and replied, 'I honestly don't know.'

Greega was still looking on, and he also expected to be cross-examined about Meidi's appalling behaviour.

Then Greega heard Laegore say, 'Sir, the incident happened yesterday after Nimra and I had finished our meal. We left the kitchen and as we walked past Meidi in the dining hall, he cleared his throat and beckoned us. The Grand Master told Nimra and I to go to his office and fetch an unopened letter stamped with a red seal. Sir, we searched high and low, but we couldn't find that particular envelope anywhere. After a while, Meidi came to his room. When he opened his door and saw us going through his desk drawer, he went ballistic.'

As Laegore spoke, Nimra remembered his terrifying beating. His mind's eye played out the frightening event and tears filled his eyes.

Laegore continued, 'Sir, you know how the Grand Master can be. It doesn't take much to provoke him. Anyway, Meidi screamed, "Get out!" Before we had a chance to leave his chambers, Meidi slammed the drawer shut, grabbed his sceptre and beat us about the head. It was a frenzied attack that happened so fast, we only protected ourselves at the last moment. Sir, I implore you not to utter a word. Like Nimra said, we don't want any comeback.'

Prince Tal was seething with anger. Nevertheless, he understood the guards' predicament and tapped them on their shoulders. 'I'll respect your wishes. Now promise me, if there's any more of Meidi's brutish behaviour, come straight to me. Do you hear?'

'Yes, Sir,' replied Nimra and Laegore.

The Prince nodded. Then he and Surrain walked across the cobbled courtyard with Veela and Sovran in tow. Prince Tal gritted his teeth and uttered, 'Damn Meidi! I won't accept his despicable behaviour. Like you, Surrain, I abhor any kind of cruelty.'

Surrain sighed. 'Do you know, now I think back, the guards' eyes have often been swollen.'

'Mm, you're right. It never occurred to me that the Dog Men were being ill-treated. I promise you Surrain, after our wedding, I'm going to get to the bottom of this abuse. It's deplorable.'

'Good,' replied Surrain. 'Meidi's got to be stopped. The power of ruling the kingdom must have gone to his head.'

As Prince Tal, Surrain and the wolves approached the entrance hall, they saw the old crones walking amongst the mortals. Igfreid held her broomstick upright and the scrawny pair pushed past Greega.

Ibsis and Igfreid, as resentful as ever, whispered to each other. A moment later, Ibsis turned round and sneered at Surrain. The old crone's top lip quivered and she expressed her feelings in her husky voice. 'We send our very own wishes to you and Prince Tal. You'll need some good luck too...he he he.'

No-one paid any attention to Ibsis, or her cynical remark.

Greega's eyes were focused on Surrain and Prince Tal, as they made their way towards him. The guard felt nervous and ran his gauntlet across his forehead, muttering to himself, 'Here we go, I'm about to be questioned.' After all his anxiety, Greega was pleasantly surprised.

Surrain was delighted to see her favourite Dog Man and smiled.

Greega bowed his head and said, 'Good day.' Then he glanced at Surrain. 'To say we were worried about you is an understatement. Now you've recovered, you're blooming like a red rose.'

Surrain chuckled. 'Thank you for the compliment, Greega. And I expect I'm red because I'm flushed with my nerves.'

Greega smiled. 'You're always happy and glowing, Surrain. That's what we Dog Men like to see. And may I offer my sincere congratulations to you both, on your forthcoming event?'

The Prince gave a nod and replied with a smile, 'Of course. And thank you, Greega. Talking about the wedding, we're here to chat to Meidi, so we'd better get a move on.'

'Do you want me to escort you to Meidi's quarters?' asked Greega.

'No we'll be fine. Carry on here. Looks like there's going to be a full house,' said the Prince, glancing at the approaching crowd. 'Besides, Surrain and I will be in my chambers before popping in to see Meidi. Then we'll make our way to the Great Hall together and watch the entertainment. You'll enjoy the show Greega. Right, my man, we must make haste.'

Prince Tal, Surrain and the two wolves made their way across the hallway, and continued on, up the winding staircase, away from the crowd. Once at the top, they turned right, towards the message table.

Veela and Sovran slowed their pace.

'Veela and I will stay here and watch the mortals, while you get ready,' said Sovran.

'OK,' said the little fairy.

Then Surrain followed Prince Tal into his chambers.

A Taste of Evil

As Surrain entered the Prince's chambers, she shivered and rubbed her arms. 'Ooh, a cold chill just ran through me...' The little fairy perched on the edge of Prince Tal's four-poster bed and sighed.

Prince Tal joined the little fairy and whispered in her ear. 'Lighten-up Surrain. Everything will be fine, I promise.'

'I hope you're right,' she replied. 'I'd better pull myself together. I'll use magic dust to create a suitable dress for the occasion. Now who are the guests?'

'Mm,' said the Prince. 'I know the sorceress will be performing, as well as introducing the acts. Wizard Jozeffri and his family will be on stage for a while. There's a jester to humour the crowd, a poet to please those who are well-read and quite a few others.'

'Well I'm not going to wear a ball-gown. I'll look stupid and overdressed.'

'No you won't, Surrain. Besides you're going to be queen of this land soon, so look the part, be distinguished. Show the mortals that you're worthy of such a title and make a good impression.'

'Oh, it's like that, is it?'

Prince Tal sighed. 'No, Surrain, it's not like that. You saw the influential mortals walk towards the entrance hall...each lady wore a fancy wig and a ball-gown'

'OK. A ball-gown it is. And if I look silly, it's your fault.' Surrain rose to her feet. She took a pinch of magic dust, uttered a spell and did a pirouette. Moments later, the little fairy stood motionless and miserable under her painted smile and brightly coloured clothes.

Prince Tal laughed aloud at her outfit. 'We don't need another jester, Surrain.'

Once again Surrain tried to carry out the desired effect. This time, the little fairy appeared scantily dressed, holding a club, wearing a leopard print covering and furry knee-high boots. As Surrain glanced at her outfit, she took a deep breath and yelled, 'Ug ug! Arghhhh...!'

Prince Tal couldn't stop laughing. Seconds later he sighed. 'OK. I've seen today's comedy act. Now stop larking about Surrain. You need to be wearing a ball-gown, so we can get going.'

Surrain used magic dust once again and repeated the procedure in her ancient tongue. She gritted her teeth. Suddenly, the little fairy began to spin round and round, until she was out of sight.

The Prince thought Surrain's silly costumes and her latest prank were intentional. Little did he know, Surrain was in dire-straits! 'Come on, Surrain, you're cutting it fine.' It wasn't long before Prince Tal realised something was wrong. He stood up and cried out, 'Surrain! Where are you?'

Surrain was on the rug near the Prince's feet. She had shrunk to the size of a house fly and the vibration of Prince Tal's voice nearly deafened her. Surrain lowered her head and placed her hands over her ears. Then the noise stopped. This was an opportunity for Surrain to get attention, so she waved her arms in the air and squeaked at the top of her voice. 'Tal, help me! Help me, I'm down here.'

Sadly, the Prince didn't see Surrain, nor did he hear her shrill cries; but an evil Gritwigg, who lived in the smut and soot of the unlit fire, heard Surrain's desperate plea for help. This long bodied insect, a monstrosity amongst its own kind, made straight for the tiny fairy. Surrain heard the insect snapping its pincer-like jaws and she turned her head. When Surrain saw the creature weaving its way towards her, a look of horror swept across her face.

This monster had a huge round head, bulging black eyes and six legs. The miniature fairy was terrified. She wasn't able to fly nor could she remember the safety spell. Surrain could only scramble over the rug and hide in its thick pile. She didn't have a chance against this ruthless beast. The snarling insect wound his segmented body along the rug and grabbed Surrain. Then the Gritwigg sunk his pincers into Surrain's delicate wings and ripped them apart.

Surrain fought for her life. She crawled, kicking and screaming, away from the creature, who began to eat her alive. All of a sudden Surrain changed form. She materialized into a miniature wolf and saved herself by devouring the evil Gritwigg.

Meanwhile, Prince Tal had reached for his amulet. He threw magic dust across the length of the rug and uttered a spell.

Almost immediately, a dishevelled wolf appeared by his side. No sooner had the Prince glanced at the wolf, when it changed form and Surrain materialized before his eyes. The little fairy, curled up and trembling, looked like a ruffled piece of tat. She had mixed emotions and laughed nervously as tears streamed down her cheeks.

Prince Tal could see how disturbed Surrain was. He knelt down beside the little fairy and wrapped his arms around her. 'Come here,' he said, trying to comfort her. 'I didn't know if you were playing games or what, but I soon realised something was wrong. What happened?'

Surrain could barely contain herself and continued to sob. After a few moments, the little fairy seemed much calmer. She looked at Prince Tal and said, 'If you only knew what I'd been through. Because I'm in poor health, I had memory loss and uttered the wrong spells. Then I shrunk and was totally helpless. Oh, Tal... Of all the creatures in this kingdom, which one frightens me the most?'

Prince Tal gazed into Surrain's watery eyes and replied, 'The Gritwigg. Why?'

'A Gritwigg wanted me for lunch. Before I lost consciousness, the horrible creature caught me and began to eat my wings. Look,' she said, and turned around.

Prince Tal shook his head and sighed, 'Oh poor you... your wings are in shreds. Let's get you up on the bed and I'll do what I can to mend them.'

'Are you using magic dust?' asked the little fairy.

'No just my hands.'

Surrain thought this was strange, as she'd never known the Prince to have any magical powers of his own. Nevertheless, with the help of Prince Tal, she climbed on the bed and lay face down. Just at that moment, Surrain began to retch... she sat up and held her throat as she heaved. To her surprise, a long mangled Gritwigg shot out of her mouth. The squirming creature wriggled through the rug, trying to escape.

Prince Tal said, 'I've just spotted the Gritwigg, Surrain.' He knelt down and grabbed the insect with a tissue. He squashed the creature and dropped the dead Gritwigg in the soot behind the grate. Then he went to wash his hands and returned to the room with a glass of water for the little fairy. 'Here you are, Surrain. Drink this down and I'll get started.'

Surrain sighed. 'Thank you. How I managed to swallow that Gritwigg is beyond me.'

'You must have gulped down the Gritwigg to protect yourself. Never mind about that now, it's gone.' The Prince rubbed his hands together and said, 'This will take no time at all. I'm going to move my hands across your shredded wings and do my best to repair them.' Within seconds the Prince had completed his task. 'That's all done, Surrain. Go and have a look in the mirror.'

The little fairy stood up and walked towards the cheval mirror. When Surrain saw her reflection, she was shocked by her dirty face and shabby appearance, yet she turned sideways, approving of her new wings. 'They're perfect. Thank you so much.' Prince Tal smiled, and Surrain asked him a question. 'That was amazing. What other powers do you possess without using magic dust?'

The Prince chuckled and replied, 'I've got healing hands... so I can purify and repair wounds, as well as cleanse a blood-soiled area, nothing more. On a change of subject, after your encounter with the Gritwigg, do you want to give our visit to Meidi a miss and go home?'

Surrain shook her head. 'No, not at all... I feel fine now. Anyway, what more could happen? I'm hoping that experience was once-in-a-lifetime.'

'Well if you're sure, Surrain.'

'Yes I'm positive. And I'm looking forward to the get-together.'

Prince Tal smiled and said, 'I'm pleased you've had a change of heart.'

Surrain made her way to the bathroom and had an invigorating wash.

When the little fairy returned to Prince Tal, he said, 'Now close your eyes and keep still.' The Prince reached for his amulet. He whispered an enchanting spell and threw a sprinkling of magic dust over Surrain. 'You can open your eyes now.'

Surrain gazed into the mirror and cried out, 'Wow, what a transformation!' Surrain rushed to the door and opened it, 'Veela, Sovran, come in and have a peek at my new look.' The little fairy twirled around as she admired her beautiful lilac ball-gown. 'What do you two think?'

Veela tilted her head and said, 'Ooh, you look wonderful Surrain.'

'I agree. You look amazing,' added Sovran.

Nothing more was said, as Veela and Sovran felt uneasy.

Surrain was so happy, she cried, 'From rags to riches, in seconds. And look at the diamond braid weaved through my curly hair. It's fabulous. Thank you, Tal.'

'You're welcome, Surrain. It's good to see you smiling.'

Surrain shivered and glanced at the Prince. 'Ooh, I just felt that cold chill again.'

Prince Tal didn't feel the iciness. He thought nothing of it and replied, 'You'll soon warm up.'

The couple embraced, not noticing a red-cloaked figure glide across the cheval mirror.

Moments later Prince Tal grabbed Surrain's hand. 'Come on. This time we Will get to our destination.'

Meanwhile, Veela and Sovran stood by the door, eager to leave the room.

Surrain glanced at her wolves and a surprised look spread across her face. 'What's the matter? Your fur is standing on end. Have you both seen a ghost?'

Veela sighed. 'We're uncomfortable, and feel ill at ease in here.'

Surrain smiled. She was oblivious to the warning signs and opened the door. 'Go on. We'll be close behind.'

Prince Tal, Surrain and an evil spirit followed the wolves out. The happy couple made their way across the landing, and noise from the bustling crowd below briefly caught their attention. The little fairy and Prince Tal were totally unaware of the dark force creeping alongside them. This eerie presence was the ferocious Crimson Cut-throat. And this time, the merciless entity aimed to satisfy his only need.

The Demon...
Up Close and Personal

Prince Tal, Surrain, Veela and Sovran were on their way to Meidi's chambers. Greega was standing a little way from the Grand Master's door, waiting for his visitors to leave.

Prince Tal approached the guard and said, 'Greega, who's in with Meidi?'

The Dog Man replied, 'Ibsis and Igfreid. But they are due out any time, Sir.'

The Prince nodded. Then he glanced at Surrain. 'We'll make our visit short and sweet.'

Just at that moment, the tittering old crones vacated Meidi's room.

When Ibsis and Igfreid reached Greega, the guard said, 'I'll escort you downstairs and to the Great Hall.'

Ibsis and Igfreid pulled their faces. They pushed past Greega and Ibsis cackled, 'Eee, we're not incompetent. Anyway, we're going home. We're not interested in those exhibitionists prancing about on stage. We've got better things to do.'

Then Igfreid waved her broom under Greega's nose. She looked up at the guard and in her husky voice she yelled, 'Yeah that's right. Move out of our way, Dog Man.'

Greega was seething with anger. He felt like whacking the sisters on top of their heads with his clenched fists, but he stood upright and calm, controlling his temper.

The Prince stepped forward and tapped Greega on his shoulder. 'Come on, my good man. Ignore those unwitting specimens. Tell Meidi I'm here with Surrain and ask him if it's convenient for us to have a quick chat.'

Greega nodded and replied, 'Right you are, Sir.'

The guard knocked on Meidi's door and he heard, 'Enter.'

After a few moments, Greega came out of Meidi's room and said, 'Sir, the Grand Master is ready to see you both. Please come this way.'

As Prince Tal, Surrain, Veela and Sovran made their way into the room, Greega promptly walked out.

The Grand Master pointed at two chairs in front of him, 'Please sit down.'

Prince Tal took hold of a wooden chair and pulled it out from under Meidi's desk. 'Here you are, Surrain. Veela, Sovran, sit in the corner, to the left of Surrain.'

Prince Tal pulled out the other chair, and sat to the right of Surrain, opposite Meidi.

The Grand Master seemed to be in good spirits. He smiled and said, 'This is a pleasant surprise. And I must say, in view of the circumstances, you look in fine fettle my dear.'

Surrain sat straight-faced. She wondered how Meidi could mistreat the guards who protected him. After hesitating, the little fairy quietly replied, 'Thank you, Meidi. I'm feeling much better now.'

The Grand Master leant over his desk and shook hands with Prince Tal. 'At last, my boy, it's time to congratulate you. Roster has done a grand job informing everyone of your wonderful news. Due to that, I've had a constant stream of well-wishers nipping in and out of here. Let's have a toast,' he said. Meidi took hold of a jug and poured frothy lichen into three goblets. 'And I'll tell you this, Tal. My visitors have given me some splendid ideas, regarding a wedding gift.'

The Prince smiled half-heartedly and said, 'I'm pleased to hear that.' Then he noticed a white diamond-studded cloak hanging at the back of Meidi's door.

The Grand Master sniggered. 'Do you like my reversible cape? Vienne has done me proud creating that unique piece of work. It's just beautiful. And today I shall hold my head high as I walk amongst those mortal peasants. Huh, primitive morons they are.' All of a sudden, Meidi banged his fist on the desktop making Surrain jump. Meidi's top lip quivered and he snarled, 'The gold braid in your hair and every glittering diamond has been obtained here, here in my kingdom. It's about time some of the resources were used.'

Meidi paused. He looked deranged, his glassy eyes widened and his head veered to the side. 'Tal, if you turn my cloak over, you'll see it's as soft as a cloud, covered with pure white feathery plumes. It's something I've always wanted.'

Prince Tal had heard enough. He thought the Grand Master was losing his mind and quickly changed the subject. The Prince reached into his breast pocket. Then he passed Meidi an unopened envelope, stamped with a red seal. 'Here you are... this is the letter you asked me to take good care of.'

Surrain frowned when she saw the envelope and thought to herself... "That's the letter Meidi wanted from his office. The red sealed envelope that caused Nimra and Laegore to be thrashed."

The Grand Master saw a certain look in Surrain's eyes and he became visibly shaken. An element of uneasiness swept across his face and his jaw dropped open. Beads of sweat covered his forehead and in a trembling voice he uttered, 'Erm... erm...' Meidi groped about in the baggy sleeve of his cassock and pulled out a crumpled hankie. He breathed deeply and wiped his brow. Then he took the envelope and shoved it into his pocket. 'Thank you, Tal.'

The Prince sighed. 'Don't look so surprised. That letter is from your brother Ker, the letter you told me to look after. Do you remember?'

Meidi sighed deeply. 'Yes...yes I do. The correspondence did escape my mind for a time, so it can't be of any importance, can it?'

Prince Tal sat upright and replied abruptly, 'I've no idea...it's addressed to you.'

Meidi continued, 'By the way, did Mr Woodrow give you the envelope?'

Prince Tal looked puzzled. 'No. The letter was handed to me by Mr Sloane. Meidi, you asked me that same question when I returned from the outside world. Am I missing something here?' he asked. The Prince took a sip of his drink.

The Grand Master fumbled through papers on his desk and replied, 'No you're not missing anything.' Meidi focussed on another matter and handed Prince Tal a few papers. 'I'd like you to read through these documents and give me your honest opinion.'

Prince Tal began to read the articles, while Surrain sat deep in thought. As Surrain gazed through the window on her left, she had a sudden urge to look at Meidi. The Grand Master's eyes were burning into Surrain and she felt extremely uncomfortable. But that was the least of her worries. Surrain saw an unforgettable sight that made her blood run cold. Meidi's features became distorted. His face broadened, and two short horns grew on his head. His beady eyes turned red and tufts of black hair sprouted out from his cheek bones. Then his mouth stretched from ear to ear, his lips became thinner and they curled back revealing short pointed teeth.

As Surrain stared, she was agitated and her throat became dry. The little fairy didn't want to say anything to Prince Tal, so instead she reached for her goblet of lichen. Surrain was about to have a drink, but when she looked into the goblet, shivers ran down her spine. There was no liquid inside the vessel, just slugs and wriggling worms. Surrain managed to keep calm. She slowly lowered the goblet, whilst staring at Meidi. Surrain couldn't take her eyes off this demon and sat paralysed with fear. The little fairy began to feel light-headed and woozy.

Then Meidi tilted his head and, without any warning, he roared at Surrain. The little fairy was so shocked by this terrifying encounter she threw herself back and crashed to the floor. Meanwhile, Veela and Sovran were already on their feet, their fur on end, snarling at Meidi. The Prince seemed oblivious to Surrain's whole experience. The little fairy looked up at Prince Tal with fear in her eyes. She asked herself, "Why isn't he responding? Is Tal ignoring Meidi's alter-ego? Or has he failed to see and hear the demon sitting before him? I know it's not my imagination. Veela and Sovran are still growling."

During this time, Prince Tal dropped the documents he was reading and helped Surrain to her feet. 'What's happened?' he cried out with concern.

Although Surrain was trembling, she kept as calm as possible. 'Nothing has happened. I leant back on the chair and lost my balance, that's all. Maybe I'm not as well as I thought,' she said, dusting down her ball-gown. After a moment Surrain turned towards Meidi, but she made a point of no eye contact. 'Please excuse me. I need some fresh air.'

The Grand Master, as normal as ever, replied, 'Certainly. I'm sorry you're not quite yourself, Surrain.'

'Let's get you out of here,' said Prince Tal, and he promptly opened the door. 'Surrain, do you want to go home and rest?'

The little fairy shook her head. 'No. I said I was going to the social gathering. Finish your business with Meidi and I'll wait here with Greega.'

'Only if you're sure, Surrain...'

'Yes, I insist.'

No Way...
Oblivious to the Damned

Surrain couldn't leave Meidi's room quickly enough. She took a deep breath and composed herself. At last Surrain was poised. She saw Greega standing a few metres away, so this was her chance to do a little digging. With Veela and Sovran by her side, Surrain made her way towards the Dog Man.

As Surrain approached Greega, he watched her every move. Greega's instincts told him something was wrong, nevertheless he stayed calm and resolute. 'Surrain, you look really lovely today, but you're extremely pale. Is there anything I can get you?' he asked.

Surrain smiled and replied, 'No thanks, Greega. I'm fine.' The little fairy then grabbed the guard's arm and whispered, 'Just walk across the landing with me. I want to ask you a question.' As Surrain and Greega approached the stairs, she leant towards the guard and whispered again, 'Tell me, have you seen or sensed any changes in Grand Master Meidi lately?'

Greega trusted Surrain, so he knew she wasn't quizzing him. But the guard trod carefully. He didn't want to disclose any information that would put himself or the other Dog Men in jeopardy. 'Funny you should ask that question,' replied Greega in his gruff voice. 'As you know, Meidi has a reputation for being angry and irritable...but today he's like a different person.'

Surrain was intrigued. 'Really?!' she exclaimed, wondering if Greega had also seen the demonic side of Meidi. 'What do you mean... a different person?'

Greega sighed, 'Well, earlier today, Wizard Jozeffri visited the Grand Master. I was standing at the foot of the stairs talking to Emnaesus, when we heard Meidi laugh and shout out, "Marvellous! Marvellous! What a brilliant idea." And when Wizard J. left the north tower, we heard Meidi singing.'

'No way... That's crazy,' giggled the little fairy.

'Huh, I can tell you this Surrain, Emnaesus and I were certainly taken aback.'

'Greega, there's something peculiar going on. I've never heard Meidi sing and he rarely laughs.'

'Don't think too much into Meidi's behaviour, Surrain. I much prefer this side of him. It must be your wedding that's cheered him up.'

The little fairy was disappointed, and thought. "Oh, Greega, if you only knew what Meidi was planning for me... Once that two-faced demon gives me a title, he's hoping I'll stay in the Realm of Elfina forever." Nor did Surrain tell the guard how Meidi exposed his alter-ego. "How would Greega understand?" she asked herself. Instead, Surrain gave the Dog Man a hug and said, 'Mm, perhaps you're right, maybe Meidi is happy about my wedding. By the way Greega, this business with Nimra and Laegore. I know you heard them chatting to the Prince earlier. Meidi is out of order, so Prince Tal will deal with the problem after our wedding.'

Greega had a worried expression and stood upright. 'I'm not sure that's a good idea, Surrain. I don't know how Meidi will react. He often loses his temper and lashes out at us Dog Men. We can't retaliate. He rules us and this land, so we have to take what he throws at us.'

Surrain looked at the guard in a sympathetic manner. 'Greega, that's where you're wrong... And don't be so anxious. You Dog Men are individuals. You all have rights. Meidi is a bully. He's taken advantage of his position and has to be stopped.' Surrain frowned. 'Has Meidi got some kind of hold over you and the other Dog Men?'

Greega sighed. He wanted to open up and tell Surrain everything, but he couldn't, this wasn't the time or place. So the guard slowly shook his head.

'I'm telling you this Greega, things around here are going to change for the better.' Surrain put her index finger over his lips and said, 'Shh. Keep quiet and trust me on this.' Then Surrain gave Greega another hug.

The guard smiled and replied, 'You can count on it.'

Just at that moment, the Grand Master's door opened.

Prince Tal walked out and said, 'Surrain, are you ready to meet your future subjects in the Great Hall?'

Surrain tried hard to smile and gulped as she made her way towards the Prince. The happy couple accompanied Meidi. They strolled down the stairs together with Greega, Veela and Sovran following closely behind.

The group walked along the dimly-lit passageway and a few mortals shuffled by. Dog Men lined the route, keeping a close eye on their shifty visitors. Surrain was feeling very nervous. The nattering crowd were filling the Great Hall, and Surrain was bracing herself for the mortal onslaught.

As they entered the Great Hall, Surrain noticed a row of tables positioned along the left side of the room. The tables were filled with an assortment of food and drink, a yearly feast for the mortals who decided to attend.

Then Meidi leant towards Prince Tal and said, 'What a sumptuous spread. In a moment I'm going to swagger down that aisle in my diamond-studded cloak and fill my belly. Just watch those mortals. They'll fall over themselves trying to compliment me. Right, I'm off.'

The Grand Master had high expectations. Meidi assumed the mortals were going to praise him as he strutted down the aisle, but at that moment, the sorceress appeared on stage and took away his moment of glory. Vienne introduced the first act and the audience applauded with excitement.

Although Veela and Sovran were by Surrain's side, she still felt uptight. The little fairy needed to find the perfect spot. Then she saw the ideal place at the back of the room. Surrain pulled on Prince Tal's arm until they were in the far right-hand corner. Surrain sighed with relief.

'Are you quite happy standing here?' asked the Prince.

Surrain smiled and replied, 'Yes, I've got a great view. I feel relaxed, so I'm going to enjoy the show.'

By now the second act had appeared on stage. This time, Vidor, Andreen and Rew were performing magic tricks. Surrain was laughing and clapping her hands. She'd already got into the swing of things. Then Vienne introduced the jester. Surrain, Prince Tal and the whole crowd roared with laughter at his wisecracks.

The Prince had his arm across Surrain's shoulder and he whispered, 'This comedian is going to be on stage for a few more minutes. I'm just going to have a word with Vienne and get a bite to eat. Do you want me to bring you something?'

'No thanks. I'm not hungry or thirsty yet. And don't rush back. I'm fine here with Veela and Sovran.'

The sorceress was standing at the left side of the stage, at the end of the long table, having a nibble.

When Surrain saw Prince Tal approach Vienne, she thought, "Ooh, I bet that's about the ancient scroll."

Prince Tal reached for a sandwich and said, 'Vienne, do you remember that musty old parchment you gave to Surrain?'

Vienne frowned, moments later she replied, 'Erm... do you mean the ancient scroll?'

'Yes I do. Where did you get it from?'

'That thing came from a large chest unearthed by two guards. I don't know where the scroll originated. All I know is I couldn't make out the symbols. Surrain liked the damn thing, so I said she could have it.'

Prince Tal shook his head. 'For goodness sake Vienne, I deciphered the ancient code instantly and understood the accursed script.'

'Good. When I have time, you can explain the system of letters and symbols to me. Then I'll have a read.'

The Prince tried to keep his cool. Nevertheless, he raised his voice and replied, 'You're right Vienne. That scroll was a damn thing...from the damned! And I made sure it was destroyed.'

At this time, Vienne didn't realise Prince Tal was talking in the past tense. She was oblivious to any danger regarding the scroll, nor was she concerned about the Prince's outburst. Vienne just lifted her hand, smiled and waved to Surrain whilst replying, 'Oh well. No harm done. Tal, it's time for me to introduce the next act. See you shortly.' When the jester left the stage, Vienne glided onto the platform. She cried out, 'Now, for those amongst us who are well-read and for poetry lovers everywhere. I present Yaarg, Prince of Bard.'

Yaarg walked on stage wearing a wide-brimmed hat, jeans, boots and a drover's coat.

When Surrain saw him, she gasped. 'No way...! If my memory serves me right, he's the man I saw leaning on a tree in the woods.'

While Surrain was thinking back, the audience went crazy, clapping their hands, whistling and shouting.

Yaarg was delighted by the warm welcome. The Prince of Bard removed his hat and held it in his outstretched arm. Yaarg bowed and said, 'Greetings Grand Master Meidi, Prince Tal, Vidor, Vienne and my fellow countrymen.' Then Yaarg stood upright and looked straight across at the little fairy. 'And not forgetting Surrain, Faerie of the Forest, our very own fair maiden, warm, gentle and kind-hearted.'

Surrain couldn't believe Yaarg had brought unwanted attention to her... She smiled nervously and nodded her head once. But in truth, Surrain wanted the floor to open and swallow her up. The adult mortals turned their heads and, for a few seconds, Surrain was gazed upon by a majority of demonic beings. It felt like forever to the little fairy, who felt a mixture of emotions.

Veela and Sovran sensed Surrain's anguish.

'Breathe deeply and ignore everyone around you,' whispered Veela.

Sovran also tried to show his support. 'Don't worry, Surrain. We're here to protect you.'

Surrain smiled at her companions, 'Thanks for the reassurance. I have faith in both of you,' she whispered.

Only when Yaarg replaced his hat and began to recite poetry, did the little fairy relax.

Surrain, along with the rest of the audience, enjoyed Yaarg's performance. Then Surrain shivered, as the dark apparition of the Crimson Cut-throat began to coil himself around her. Veela and Sovran sensed an evil presence. Even though the wolves were uneasy and troubled by this spirit, they couldn't see the apparition to warn Surrain.

When Yaarg left the stage, the crowd applauded and shouted, 'More! More! More!'

Surrain smiled. Once again the sorceress appeared on stage and the crowd calmed down. Then Vienne introduced a truly magical act, Wizard Jozeffri, his wife Marion and their son Casey.

Coloured ribbons and balloons suddenly swept over the heads of the audience. Moments later the ribbons vanished, and, as each balloon exploded, white doves appeared. The birds changed form and the crowd watched in awe, as silver stars rained down upon them. Then Wizard J. appeared and the audience applauded. The crowd enjoyed every breathtaking moment of magic he threw at them.

Surrain was intrigued and totally absorbed by the performance. Then Yaarg materialized beside Surrain. 'Hello, doll.'

Surrain was surprised by Yaarg's sudden appearance. She stepped back and gasped, 'Where did you spring from?'

'Ah ha!' replied Yaarg.

'What sort of reply is that?' cried Surrain. 'Oh, and thanks for embarrassing me. I love to be gazed at by those demonic morons.' Surrain frowned, 'I remember you from the woods. You just vanished into thin air.'

Yaarg sniggered, 'Ah, so I did. Surrain, we were acquainted long before you saw me in the woods.'

'Well I don't recall ever seeing or speaking to you.' Surrain sighed deeply and tutted. 'And I'd be grateful if you wouldn't creep up on me. I'm liable to lash out.'

Yaarg didn't reply. He glanced down at the white marble floor and back up at Surrain. 'Don't worry, you'll be fine.'

The little fairy sighed and thought, "What is he talking about now?" Surrain whispered to Yaarg, 'You do annoy me when you talk in riddles. Will you go away before the mortals see you? Like I said a short time ago, I don't want to be stared at by a room full of demonic faces. Why don't you go and speak to Tal?'

'No. He's backstage chatting to Meidi and the sorceress. And that's just what we are doing, except we are standing here.'

Surrain's patience was wearing thin and she sighed again. Then something caught her eye. The little fairy glanced to her left. A few seconds later Surrain turned round, and Yaarg was gone.

While Surrain had been talking to Yaarg, Wizard Jozeffri and Casey amazed their audience with their dazzling magic. Jozeffri and Casey stood at opposite ends of the stage facing each other. Wizard J. moved his hands from side to side and a magical beam of colours appeared from his palms. The radiating colours, along with six baubles, shot across the stage and wound round Casey. The beam rose up and burst into coloured stars, falling between J. and Casey. As the mesmerised crowd watched, the stars materialized into

Marion. She held three adorable kittens in her open hands and glanced at her son. On Casey's outstretched arms sat two tortoiseshell cats, Chuchie and Trixie, while Wizard J. held Ling. The audience applauded as they uttered, 'Aw,' but the show wasn't over. All six cats proceeded to stand upright on one leg and they spun round in a pirouette. After a number of turns, the smiling cats bowed, and gave themselves a round of applause. The crowd couldn't believe their eyes. They cried out with joy and clapped their hands at the spectacular performance. Vienne noticed a look of wonder spread across Surrain's face and had an idea. Then Wizard J. and his family began to change form. Their bodies turned as if on an axis, and the family materialized into grey mist. The hazy clouds suddenly spun towards each other and, as the whirling mass touched, the magical threesome, along with their six cats, vanished.

Once again Vienne stepped onto the stage and introduced another act.

During the hearty laughter, Surrain shivered. The little fairy felt compelled to look towards her left again. For a moment, Surrain thought her eyes were deceiving her; but as she gazed above the long table, Surrain saw the Grim Reaper and his horse appear, halfway up the wall. The little fairy blinked twice, to make sure she wasn't seeing things. As Surrain stared, the Grim Reaper turned his ghostly horse towards her, and rode over the heads of the unsuspecting crowd.

Surrain had to move fast. She crouched down, whispering to Veela and Sovran. 'Keep as calm as you can and stay close. The Grim Reaper and his horse are riding through mid-air, straight for us. We're going to leave here without anyone noticing, and make a dash for Tal's room. Got it?'

Although Veela and Sovran were fraught with fear, they nodded in response.

Surrain, Veela and Sovran left the Great Hall. The wolves made a run for it, while the little fairy fluttered her wings and took off. As the ghostly horse and rider pursued the terrified trio, Surrain panicked and lost her way. The little fairy turned down the wrong passage and flew deep into the bowels of Magentis Castle. While the sound of pounding hooves echoed along the dark eerie passages, bats and sinister shadows flitted from wall to wall; squealing rats ran amok and dripping water trickled down the damp stone walls. Surrain flew on, but her health rapidly deteriorated. The little fairy couldn't take much more. Surrain landed in the centre of the passage, behind her wolves. To Veela and Sovran's horror, Surrain turned and faced her oncoming demon.

'Take Me! Take Me Now...You Dumb Ass Entity. Just leave my loved ones alone!' yelled Surrain.

The Grim Reaper's horse came to a grinding halt close to Surrain... Veela and Sovran leapt at the horse and snapped ferociously at the animal's back legs. The wolves tried to protect the little fairy, but their efforts were in vain. It was a hopeless task against a demonic horse. The huge beast kicked out maiming Veela and Sovran... nevertheless the injured wolves continued snarling.

Meanwhile, the Crimson Cut-throat materialized behind Surrain. This evil ghoul was ready to take the little fairy's life, but as the Grim Reaper was Chief Soul Taker, the Crimson Cut-throat hesitated.

As the horse reared up, the Grim Reaper waved his scythe high above his head, whilst roaring, 'Arghhhhhhh.'

Surrain froze, and watched in terror as the curved blade glided through the air, towards her. Veela and Sovran couldn't do any more to protect Surrain. This time, the little fairy was struck, and her frail body fell against the cold, damp, stone wall.

Lightning Source UK Ltd.
Milton Keynes UK
UKOW07f1808191114

241866UK00016B/517/P